ELLE HARTFORD

The Silver Deck

A Leonine Investigations Mystery

Phoenix & Kelpie

First published by Phoenix & Kelpie Press 2025

This novel is entirely a work of fiction. The names, characters and incidents portrayed in it are the work of the author's imagination. Any resemblance to actual persons, living or dead, events or localities is entirely coincidental.

Elle Hartford asserts the moral right to be identified as the author of this work.

First edition

ISBN: 979-8-9921588-3-0

This book was professionally typeset on Reedsy.
Find out more at reedsy.com

Contents

Contents

1

A Card Above

Everyone else in Belville got roses and love letters for Valentine's Day. I got a hanged man.

Not that I'm complaining.

It was *the* Hanged Man, if I'm going to be specific. Makes a difference, doesn't it?

I went into the office that day like usual. There was snow on the ground and winter still in the air. The print shop windows open out onto Market Square, and I could see people in bright red caps and scarves amid heart decorations hanging from the trees. All that red and white had me thinking about murder in print.

You really can't blame me. Murder does sell papers. And the holiday season had been glacially slow, as far as news was concerned.

So there I was, alone at headquarters. I'd climbed the dusty stairs, passed the printing presses and turned into the back room—the one office: my office. I dumped the mail on my desk and tossed my coat over an old chair. And as I was reaching for my printer's apron, I saw that one of the envelopes in the mail had opened.

It had fallen apart from the others. When I leaned in, I could tell that it had never been sealed. It was just a plain white envelope, no stamp. More interesting was the card that had slipped out. It was the size of a normal playing card, but there was nothing normal about it. The paper was thick, shiny, and black as black could be. Details had been added in silver. Inside a thin frame, a depiction of a person dangling by one foot from a tree over a wild stream stared up at me.

The person's arms were crossed and their hair hung down into the water. The face looked . . . resigned.

I stared at it for a good two minutes before I decided to risk picking it up. *Pen and ink are the mightiest weapons out there,* as my grandda said. He'd have turned over in his grave if he saw me lay hands on an unknown card. It could have been cursed, for all I knew.

But I couldn't resist.

I'd never seen a card like it before. It wasn't your usual doily-covered Valentine. I checked the rest of the envelope, but it was empty. Nothing of note in the rest of the mail, either. I flopped down behind the desk and studied the card again. What could it mean?

Technically I should have been working on the paper's special Valentine's Day report. It was always a good seller. But it was also the same stuff every year. This card was something new. I tapped it against my desk as I thought.

Finally I threw the card down and decided to look into how it had got to me. The window in my office looked out over the back of the building, into the alley. From my flat on the second floor, I could just barely see the mailbox and the back entrance. I had to rub my breath off the panes to get a good look. There were clearly just two sets of prints in the snow: mine, and the mail carrier's. I could tell the prints were hers because they meandered down the alley, stopping at every mailbox behind the buildings lining Market Square.

So, no one had come up to the print shop's mailbox in person to deliver the note—at least, not on two feet. Or any feet for that matter.

Across the alley a shadow moved, catching my attention. A row of houses stood opposite my window, and behind one of those houses, a creature crept. It looked no bigger than a badger, maybe as tall as my knee. I'm regrettably short. I pulled back stray curls so I could get closer to the window. *Like a nest of auburn springs,* that's how my granda described my hair. With my free hand, I groped for my hat to control the mess. I had to see what was in the alley. It seemed to have wings.

Then it looked straight up at me, through the dirty glass.

I could see its glowing eyes.

In a whirlwind of black feathers, it shot into the air and straight at me. Claws and fangs hit my window. I fell back over the arm of my desk chair, cap falling to the ground. Snow off my boots was everywhere. There was a screeching and a scrabbling, and my own heavy breath.

And then just like that it was gone.

I pulled myself up in the chair, wincing as my back ached where it'd hit the desk. I scooped up my cap and jammed it on top of my head and my eyes fell on that little black card.

The Hanged Man, it said, in delicate silver lettering, underneath the numeral XII.

Obviously that creature had flown to my mailbox and left this card there. And now it was harassing me. If there's one thing I won't stand, it's being bullied.

3

I snatched up the card and my coat and ran down the stairs.

* * *

I spent all morning tracking that animal through snow and ice.

The first step was easy. I found a loose black feather at the end of the alley. It was the size and shape of a raven feather, but I knew better. The beast that had bared its fangs on my window had been no raven.

The next step was more difficult. Based on the feather, I knew that the creature had flown to Market Square for cover. But when I questioned the civilians no one could give me a lead. All they wanted to talk about was who sent whom a secret admirer note and who had completed a "love quiz."

Sometimes, the bystanders of Belville are useless.

I got a break in the case when I stopped for coffee. Like everything else of any importance in town, the café is right on Market Square. From its front windows, I could see my print shop—tucked above an art store—in a corner to the right. While I was observing the view and sipping on my extra-dark-chocolate-hold-the-whipped-cream-hold-the-sprinkles, I saw that cursed black shadow again.

It was fast, but I was faster. Without bothering with a lid for my ceramic to-go cup, I threw my long coat back on and darted out the door. Porch furniture festooned with pink ribbons in front of the café slowed me down, but I kept my eye on the prize. I shook my foot free of a particularly in-the-way chair and raced back to headquarters.

The creature had flown up and disappeared into the roof line. I knew what to do. Most of the buildings around Market Square were that old blocky style, two or three stories of brick and wood under steep roofs and chimneys. The building that housed the art shop and my print shop was freestanding, but I could get to the roof via the third floor, which was a maze of cobwebs and forgotten storage. Maybe I could ask the landlords downstairs about using that as a repair space for the printing presses . . .

I found the hatch I needed and shoved it open. A wooden staircase unraveled in a cloud of dust. It was barely hanging on by a string, but I made it up quick. It led me into the forgotten attic.

I had to remember my way through a series of rooms, ducking under beams where the peaks in the roof dipped down. Who knows why the original owners had built their top floor like some sort of sadistic trap. What had they kept up there?

I finally found the window I wanted and forced it open. I had to push hard because of the weight of the snow against the frame. Sunlight met the gloom as I poked my head out. From there, I could climb onto the roof and round the corner, and I'd be looking right over Market Square. A series of railings and gargoyles would keep me from sliding below.

I made my way out carefully. My boots were sturdy on the roof tiles, even in the snow, but the last thing I wanted was to startle the creature. It obviously had a hiding spot nearby. Even if it had heard me coming, it was probably absorbed in its evil work. It could have been sabotaging a chimney, or plotting to knock one of the gargoyles onto a passerby, or eating roof tiles for lunch. Whatever it is that these creatures do.

I rounded the corner and took a look around. From there, I was looking right into the tops of the trees in Market Square. The roof itself was fairly boring, stretches of white snow waiting to slide down at any moment. The valleys between the steep angles were full of ice and powder. But over by the chimney, I spotted a dark area. I made my way through a valley to investigate.

The dark area had been wiped clean of snow. It had been built as a ledge supporting the chimney. But it was clearly in use for other purposes. Tufts of black fluff and the smell of fish met me as I leaned in. It was a secluded spot, tucked between the chimney and the steepest part of the roof. There was good shelter from the wind. I was just regretting having dropped my drink in the alley when I heard the scratch of nails on metal.

Instantly I turned. There, on the highest peak of the roof, clinging to the weather vane, was the creature.

It screeched at me and I fell back against the chimney for support. I pulled the black card from my pocket and held it out in front of my face.

"I know what you've been doing!" I yelled.

The suspect screeched again and swiped at the card.

That made me pause. Why would it want to destroy the card it was using to harass *me*?

Was it trying to destroy evidence?

"I can prove it with or without the card," I added for good measure. "I found your lair!"

The creature yowled. My foot slipped over the tiles, sending me down sideways. I hit the chimney ledge with a hard *oof* as my breath left me. Most of my weight was on my left elbow. For a moment I could see stars.

And then I saw hearts. The garlands and flags on the tree limbs below. *Quite* far below.

Fiddlesticks. I could hear grandda say it in my head.

* * *

6

I'm not sure how long I leaned there on that ledge, three and a half stories up. At least I'd managed to pull myself into a more sturdy sitting position. When I could breathe normally again, there was frost on my coat and my stomach was rumbling.

And there was a cat on my head.

It purred from its position, its claws digging into my cap.

"When did *this* happen?" I asked the world in general. I brandished the only thing I had: that little black card. The glint of the silver lettering caught my eye, and I studied it again.

Funny how much being stuck on a roof can feel like hanging upside down from a tree.

Above me, the cat meowed.

I reached up and grabbed it, pulling it down into my lap. It protested and won my cap in the struggle. Finally we sat face to face, both disheveled.

"Black cat with raven wings," I said out loud, just to make sure it was true. The creature in question glared at me with glowing silver eyes. "Yeah, you're definitely bad luck."

It had led me onto a roof, after all. But I had to admit it wasn't totally guilty. "I'm guessing by your reaction earlier that you didn't send me this card?" I asked, holding up the Hanged Man.

The cat looked at it and hissed.

"Yeah. You don't seem to have many envelopes up here, either," I decided. "So it wasn't you, then. Truce?"

The cat looked away, its chin in the air.

I looked too. "Do you *live* up here?"

A look of disdain from the cat.

I tried again. "Do you *like* it up here?"

The cat shifted uncomfortably on top of my smushed cap.

"Okay then. I'm assuming you can understand me," I informed it. "And if you can, then I propose a deal. You show

7

me how to get out of here, and I'll get the landlords to let you live in the attic. It's got to be better than the roof. It'll get hot here in the summer."

The cat slowly blinked at me.

"Fine. The third floor?"

The cat stretched, digging its gleaming claws deeper into my cap, and then flapped off with its abnormal wings. It circled the smaller roof line and came back, eyeing me from a snowdrift.

"If you say so," I muttered, jamming my cap back over my hair. If I was going to make it without slipping again, I would need to focus.

It was a longer journey getting back than going out. But credit where credit is due: that cat got me back to the attic window. Then it stuck to me like glue until I'd shimmied down the ladder to the third floor. We stood there in the dust looking at each other.

I looked at my card again.

"Here I am still stuck with a mystery that isn't fit to print," I murmured to myself. "And stuck with a flying cat to boot."

I tried to close the door to my office, to think things over and plan my next step. But the silver-eyed cat followed me in.

* * *

8

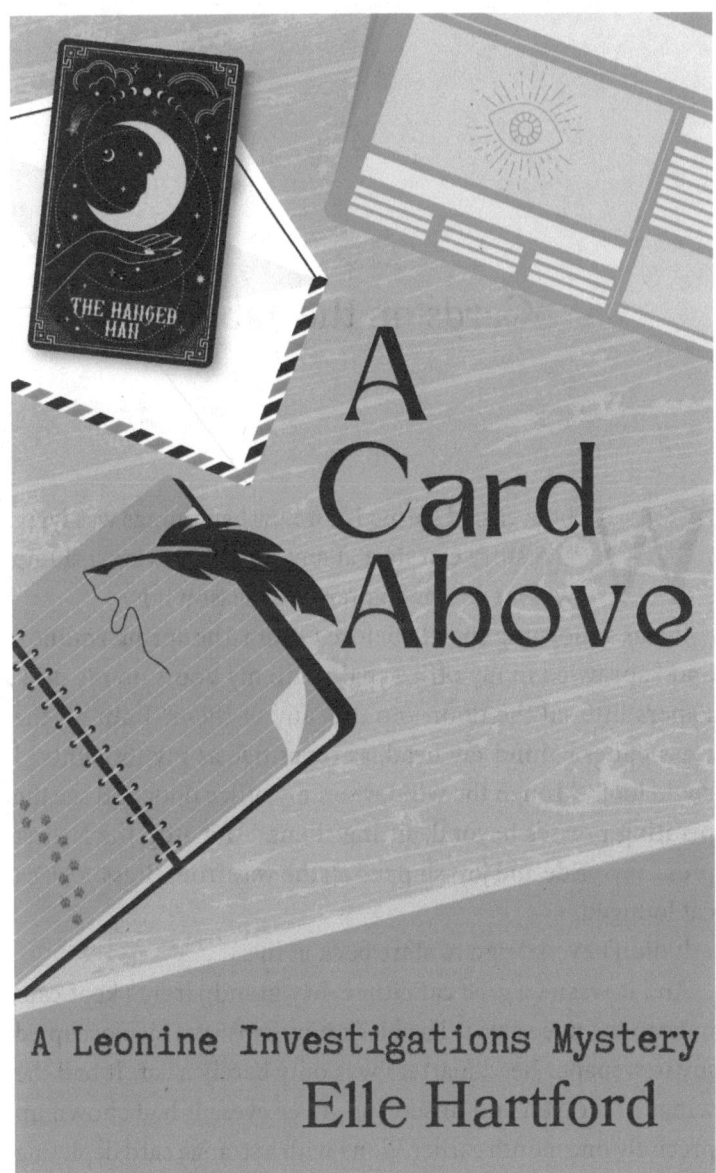

A
Card
Above

A Leonine Investigations Mystery
Elle Hartford

2

Cards on the Table

Whoever said spring is for new beginnings was lying. A story can start at any time. Likewise, a slump will hit you no matter what season it is.

It was a morning shortly before Ostara, the spring equinox, and I sprawled in my office chair with my boots on my desk. Papers littered the floor—no use, any of them. Rain hit the glass panes behind my head, as repetitive as my thoughts. I could look through the window on my office door and see the printing presses beyond, sitting silent. And atop the largest press, my pride and joy, shipped all the way from Brass, a black cat lounged.

It didn't even deign to stare back at me.

And it wasn't a *good* cat either. My grandparents kept cats, to keep the mice away. The black monstrosity which occupied my newspaper headquarters was only barely a cat. It had the wings of a raven and unsettling silver eyes. It had shown up precisely one month earlier, along with a strange card depicting a "Hanged Man." I had yet to determine if cat and card were related.

And in the day's mail, another card had arrived.

The new card wasn't as graphic as the first. And yet it was still unsettling. Shiny black cardstock sported an etched, metallic illustration of a large wheel. The kind used for carts—or for torture, in bygone days. The card bore the numeral X and the title "Wheel of Fortune."

No one ever got tortured in Belville these days. Unless you counted coerced volunteerism at town events.

Still, I knew a mystery when I saw one. My reporter's senses were tingling.

And the cat was ignoring me.

I *could* have shooed it off the presses and got to work, of course. But card or no, the news around town was uninspired, and so was I.

Footsteps sounded on the stairs. The newspaper headquarters sat above an art shop, and sometimes people dropped by to place an ad—but that was rare. Most often people found me while I was out reporting instead of braving the alley and the stairs to visit the office.

The cat and I watched the outer door. When it opened, a stranger stepped in. A stranger even newer than my infernal cat.

I pulled my boots off my desk and perked up a little.

The stranger hesitated, like he was leaving something in the hall. Then he spotted my office—it's the only one—and pushed the door open, pausing to read off the plaque. "Mary Jane Leonine?"

"Leo," I corrected, tipping my cap up over my curls to get a good look at him. His dark suit was dry, his nice new umbrella dripping, black hair slicked back and pale face smiling. Either he was here to place an ad, or he was about to be disappointed.

"Ah, yes, Leo—I've already heard your name around town," he said, claiming the one other chair in the office. He couldn't have been any taller or weigh any more than I did, and I'm short and stocky. But he spoke with a big personality. "They say this is the place to come to get acquainted with everything there is to know about Belville."

I narrowed my hazel eyes. "This is no tourist stop."

"Oh, I don't want to know the *tourist* details," he replied, with just the right amount of derision. "I'm here for the juicier stories. Call me Patty. Am I interrupting your tarot reading?"

He pointed carelessly at the card, which sat atop a pile of opened mail. I frowned as I tucked it into a pocket. I didn't know much about tarot, and I didn't like being at a disadvantage. "Just an inside joke."

"I must say, your coworker doesn't seem the joking type," said Patty. He gestured through the window over his shoulder at the cat. The cat was still ignoring me—staring at the stairway door. Patty apparently *was* the joking type, though. He leaned over my desk and added, "I travel with a bird, myself. But when I saw your cat, I thought it better to leave mine outside."

"Not mine," I said. Just a reflex. Animals were common enough companions in Beyond. And if he had a bird outside, that explained the cat's behavior. For the moment, at least. "If you're looking for stories—"

"My dear editor," Patty interrupted, smiling again, "I am here for gossip. How many back issues do you have on hand?"

I hesitated. He was staring at my right hand. The burnished copper never quite matched my tan skin. Not that I ever tried to hide the prosthetic—but I didn't like drawing attention, either.

"Please excuse me. I didn't mean to be rude—I simply could help but admire the handiwork," Patty said. He seemed genuine.

And my false hand *was* made by the best tinkerers in Beyond, so he was right. I shrugged off the interaction, and he went on. "I came here hoping to stock up on local news, you see. I always find it's best to do some research when you come into a new town, don't you?"

He'd pulled out a thick wallet as he spoke. Through the sparkle of a tamper-proof fairy charm, he pulled out several bills, indicating he was prepared to pay for the papers.

That bit of respect went a long way toward turning my mood around. As I turned to the filing cabinets along one wall, I agreed with him. "Research is always a good idea."

* * *

Research is exactly what I'd been missing.

When the cat first showed up, of course I'd canvassed the neighborhood. I am a reporter, after all. But no one I'd interviewed had known anything about the creature—and nothing about the mysterious card, either. The entire neighborhood behind the print shop, not to mention the block of businesses on either side, and not a single lead.

I'd paused to reassess my situation after that. Especially because by then, the cat had wormed its way into my headquarters, instead of staying in the attic like it was supposed to.

Now it was clearly time for round two. Instead of going door to door, I went for the heart of the matter.

The newspaper office sits at one corner of Market Square, Belville's tiny business district and town park. Heading due south toward the neighboring corner, I hit Lavender's Tavern.

A long wooden building with blooming flower boxes and a wraparound balcony, it didn't look like much. But Lavender's was the center of town. The drinks were good, and the gossip even better. I often stopped by the bar on my way home. Most strangers stayed in the rooms upstairs, so it was always the first place for news about comings and goings.

I got there just after the lunch rush and ordered my usual cider before pulling out my notebook. I laid it to the left of my glass, ready for anything. Years ago I'd taught myself to write quickly and left-handed. Printing accidents were no joke.

Once I'd set up, I knew it wouldn't take long before Lavender came over. I'd never known her to take a day off. She seemed to love every single moment on the job, though. She was tall, large, and her long silver hair occasionally sported a feather or two. There was plenty of speculation about that, but I knew better than to print it. You stay in business by knowing who your friends are.

"Leo, you're in early," said the woman herself, appearing from the kitchen. "Ready for the Ostara Fair?"

Not hardly. The town's egg hunt ranked among my least favorite holidays. But I kept that to myself. "Actually, Lavender, I'm here to see you about a cat. And a card."

"Always cool and focused, aren't you." She settled against the counter, purple eyes gleaming. "Do tell."

I described the cat and both cards to her in detail. By the end of it, though, I was no wiser. Lavender had no clues to give me. She did, however, give me a slice of cake.

And on her way back into the kitchen, she tossed a piece of advice over her shoulder. "Tarot is all about metaphor, dear. It won't tell you anything you don't already know."

I knew nothing about this case so far, so that made no sense.

For my next stop, I decided to be more practical. There was one vet in Belville, and so far, I'd avoided them like the

14

plague. The last thing I needed was actual cat ownership and responsibility. But needs must, as my Granda would say.

I went in with my notebook ready and my questions set.

I came out with a pile of magical cat books, a brochure on town pet policy, a purple collar, and a bag of specialty flying cat food. I hadn't even known half those things existed.

And I knew that if I tried applying the collar, I'd lose fingers.

But the books were promising. And despite the cider earlier, my throat was parched. Due to repetition of *no, it's really not my cat,* no doubt. No matter—the Pomegranate Café was nearby.

I ducked into the café, shaking rain off my boots. After a brief stop at the counter to get my usual large coffee extra black, I found the quietest spot I could. A little table on the second floor balcony suited me fine. In no time, I was deep into my assigned reading.

Cabbits, cactus cats, carbuncles. Who knew so many kinds of magic cat existed?

I was up to my ears in cat classifications. Most were unhelpful, and none mentioned a penchant for springing tarot cards on unsuspecting victims. Familiars, butter cats, wampus cats. Nothing fit the bill. And none of it made sense combined with a "Hanged Man" or a "Wheel," either.

Somewhere in the muddle, I was interrupted by another local. Red, a meddlesome alchemist. General consensus was that she was handy with a potion, but she could get her knickers in a twist easily and rarely made a good witness for the paper. I hardly paid mind to what she said—something about the Ostara fair (curse it).

But when I'd drained my coffee, I remembered: Red *had* a familiar. She always insisted that he wasn't hers, of course, but that didn't matter. I resolved to stop by the potions shop to learn more about him.

Turned out I didn't even have to go that far. He tripped me up as I left the Pomegranate.

"Leo. On a case?" he commented wryly. With blue magic, he held my spilled books aloft.

"Paper business," I confirmed, snatching the books out of the rain. Wryness was William's stock in trade. Truth be told, I liked him. And unlike my unusual cat, he looked like a perfectly normal—if wolfish—large black dog. Until he busted out the magic or started talking, that is.

"Try an article on paying attention where you're going," he suggested.

I ignored the joke. "This is more important. I was just coming to find you."

"Me?" William followed me away from the café door. We stood on its little porch, huddling under cover from the rain. "Well, you found me."

"Yes, and I need your opinion." As quickly as I could, I gave him the rundown on the strange cat and the tarot cards.

William sat and tilted his head to the side. I realized that now that I'd said something to him, it'd probably be all over town. But that was the least of my problems.

"I haven't *seen* what you're describing, but I *have* sensed a new presence over at the art building," he admitted after a moment.

I shifted my books to pull out my notebook. "The cat? You can sense the cat? Or—something more sinister?"

"Nothing sinister," William said dryly. "Most likely, it's just marking out its territory."

I lowered my notes. "Not—my shop?"

"Can't imagine why. Those presses make a racket," William panted. "But it looks to me like you have a new roommate."

16

"Not if it's trying to terrorize me with tarot cards," I retorted.

"Are you really terrorized, though?" he asked. "That doesn't fit the hard-nosed reporter persona."

I shifted. "Of course not. But they *are* threatening."

"Vaguely," William agreed. It was clear he doubted me, but I ignored his editorializing. "If you ask me though, magic or no, your new guest is more likely to deliver a message to you via dead mouse. It is a *cat,* after all."

* * *

Our next sunny day was Ostara. Sometimes, the weather is *too* predictable.

I'd had a few days to think since my latest lead. But I had to admit, the cat research had turned up nothing.

It had been a momentary high—thinking I might be on to something. Instead, I was just as stumped as before. And now I was manning a booth at a raucous Ostara fair handing out egg-themed crosswords, to boot.

Strangely enough, the cat had decided to join me. It had been enjoying the flying cat food—*someone* might as well eat it. No mice had turned up on my desk, and no more tarot cards in the mail, either.

I leaned my head in one hand as I sat behind my table. A granny came up for the free special-edition Ostara newspaper. The cat fluttered down from the tent beams overhead to hand it to her. I sighed. In a few hours' time I'd have to pay attention to the egg hunt, so I could write up a proper report later. Things like that did sell papers in Belville . . . but I preferred the kind of publicity that came from covering exciting cases.

And here I was with a case involving *me,* and no clue what to do about it.

Before I could get lost in my thoughts, there was a commotion at the center of the Square. The Fair was kicking off with a talent show, complete with a makeshift stage in the park. From my booth at the edge of the green, I could barely see what was going on. A cloud of chickens had erupted onto the crowd. Someone was shouting. William and his friend Red dove off the stage.

I stood. If Red and William were involved, then this might be newsworthy trouble.

Fowl assault or no, the citizens of Belville were a determined audience. I had to push my way to get within earshot of the action. A wet chicken shot past me and I knocked into a large, orcish lady. She set me back on my feet with a friendly smile. I pulled my cap down over my curls and pulled my notebook out. *Pay attention to where you're going,* William had said. Well, I wasn't going to miss this!

The crowd was murmuring, but their attention was still focused on the stage. There, the stranger from before—Patty—was shouting about gold and hoaxes with the tone of an expert. He was flying as he spoke, hovering on large green fairy wings. I tried to pick up the thread of what he was saying, something about riches and envy, but got knocked aside again. The town bookseller raced past with a chicken under each arm.

This was getting ridiculous.

"Get him," a farmer next to me shouted.

"Pin him down!" another nearby agreed.

I couldn't have agreed more. Maybe I should have expected such mayhem—it *was* a Belville holiday, after all. But I hated the feeling of being literally on my back foot.

Unexpectedly, just then, someone *did* "get him." A small, lithe

18

person I recognized from the hair salon leapt from the stage curtains and swung from Patty's feet. The town Witch captured them both in a strand of magic, and they were lowered onto the stage.

I scribbled notes furiously, knowing I could look up names and background information later. Quick as a cat, Belville's local police officer, Thorn, arrested Patty. For no less charge than fraud and harassment!

He *had* had that air of the con man when he'd stopped by the newspaper office. And no wonder he had come to see me first—he'd wanted to get on the good side of the paper, no doubt.

As Officer Thorn and the Witch brought Patty off stage, I fought my way through the crowd. I was determined to get in that interview. Officer Thorn ignored me at first, even when I finally caught up with them at the police station, a few blocks from the Square. But she knew me well. Eventually, she relented.

"You can have a few moments while I finish up the paperwork," she told me. "If he says anything useful, you let me know."

I saw my chance and took it before she could change her mind. I darted down the stairs to the basement of the station, where Patty sat in a cell.

"Ah, the reporter," he said, pausing in his rant at the Witch, who was finishing up the spells that would keep him in place. "Where's your cat?"

That dratted cat. It had thrown me so far off my game. There I was, all set for an exclusive jailhouse interview, and I blurted out the first thing that came to mind. "Why did you think the cat would have had something to do with the cards?"

"Did I?" Patty looked as thrown as I was. It was the *least* relevant question to the situation. I'd totally lost my cool.

And yet—it got his attention. "If anyone should have anything to do with that tarot card, it'd be a gem smith. To etch it with silver like that—what kind of cat has access to such fine ores?"

What kind, indeed. I gaped. Then regained control. "Is that your professional opinion as a mineral fraudster?"

"Now you see here, missy," he said, glaring through the bars. "Nothing about anything I've done is fraud—they're setting me up—*they* are the fraudsters!"

No good confidence trickster would ever admit to the con. My Granda always said as much, and it was true. I'd met the type occasionally as a reporter. They weren't as uncommon as you'd think.

I fired a few more questions at him and got some good pull quotes for the paper, but nothing of real use. Finally, Officer Thorn and her witchy friend decided it was time we all went back to the fair.

The egg hunt was starting soon.

My resistance to watching the town kiddies hunt eggs had waned, though. I now had something more interesting to think over. A new lead . . .

Back at my booth, I pulled the Wheel of Fortune card out of my pocket. The sunshine fell straight across my table, not entirely blocked by the tent. As I turned the card back and forth in my copper hand, the silver gleamed.

I looked over at the cat. It was sitting in the basket which once held the Ostara crossword puzzles. As usual, it was completely uninterested.

But *I* was feeling interested again. Interested in the case. I looked at that sparkling wheel on the cardstock. It was just like my investigation so far: turning down, then up, then down and up again.

The thought sent a shiver down my spine. Whoever was sending these cards knew me *far* too well.

* * *

Cards on the Table

A Leonine Investigations Mystery

Elle Hartford

3

Card Shark

A diamond in the rough might be hard to find, but a lead in a mine was easy.

I knew exactly where to go next on the tarot card case.

I started my day at the newspaper headquarters, as usual. The winged black cat, Nyx, yawned as she watched me dump my lunchbox and bag on my office desk before switching out my raincoat for a collared jacket. Spring weather in Belville was nice enough for the birdwatchers, but not so good for anyone out for a climb.

After the last tip about the mysterious tarot cards—that the silver etching was the mark of a professional—I'd prepared an arsenal of information. Every moment I wasn't reporting or printing the town's paper, I'd been chasing down details about the mines in the area. Belville was square in the middle of a mountain range, so there was no shortage of those. First and foremost on the list was the Belville Mountain mine. Just a short jaunt up the cliffs, and yet untouchable . . . until now.

I tightened the laces on my boots and pulled my cap down

tighter over my auburn curls. The thing about Belville's hometown mine was that it wasn't just professional, it was elite. Not because of its workforce, technology, or product—I'd written enough stories about miners brawling and suspicious ore to know that. But the lady running it all was a force to be reckoned with. Not many people in small town Belville made me nervous. She did.

Tucking my notebook and pencil in my breast pocket, I was ready to go. I slipped the two mysterious tarot cards I'd received so far into an inner pocket, just in case. My notebook was full of notes on mine dealings and local minerals. The crowning jewel of it all: in my research, I'd discovered that the mine did have one weak spot—a dangerous dragon that lived on the mountain. A dragon they certainly wouldn't want some nosy reporter stirring up.

If she thought she could intimidate me without consequence, she had another think coming.

I swung my office door closed. Nyx was asleep on one of the printing presses on the main floor, as usual. She showed no interest in coming along. I might have liked the company, but decided I was better off alone anyway.

After locking up headquarters with the cat inside, I ran down the stairs. Coming out into the alley, I nearly ran right over the local postmaster.

"Oh, Leo," she said, stepping out of the way just in time. "You're out early. There's just one letter for you today. Someone must have hand-delivered it—it was already in the mailbox when I checked for outgoing mail."

She handed me a plain little envelope that stopped me in my tracks. I mumbled out some pleasantries. I wasn't about to tell a civilian about the tarot cards. She'd already told me time and again that she knew nothing about personal deliveries.

No one in Belville seemed to know anything. Especially about these cards. As the postmistress walked on, I snuck a glance inside the envelope. As I'd expected, it held one black playing card, etched in silver with an illustration of a witch pointing up with one hand and down with the other.

"The Magician," it read. Pointing in opposite directions was a pretty good summary of my experience with magic as a reporter, I'd say. Myself, I preferred technology.

Either way, I wasn't going to be deterred now.

I tucked the card into my pocket with the others.

* * *

Half an hour later, I'd huffed up the mountain and arrived at the mine.

The road from the mine into town was rough dirt. Not a great prospect for making a quick getaway. Not to mention that the forest was thick on one side of the road. The tree trunks were like massive sentries. The mine itself was set into a canyon in the mountain, guarded on the back and sides by heaps of stone. The chasm walls met the road like the maws of a great beast.

But I hadn't come up all this way just to run off. I squared my shoulders and marched in.

The mine's headquarters was a wooden building no bigger than my print shop, right at the center of the operation. It wasn't fancy, but it demanded respect. Passing mine carts and crossing over the mine's rail line to get there reminded me that I was walking into a powerful operation. No doubt that's exactly the impression Lark wanted to give.

I showed up at their door with dust on my boots and iron in my spine.

A secretary met me in the front room. I hadn't come across him before. It had been a while since I'd visited the mine, though. It was clear from his quick movements that he'd been there a while. He gestured with one hand for me to sit while simultaneously using the other to wave through the interior door. At about five foot, even shorter and much more slender than me, he made an interesting change from the mine's previous "secretaries," a pair of trolls.

The trolls had been chatty, though. This one wouldn't even look me in the face while I waited. So I kept my silence.

When at last he let me into the main office, I made a point to shut the door behind me.

Shutting the door gave me a moment. I needed one. Seeing Lark always set my nerves buzzing.

She was a coastal elf, with the classic sand-colored skin and ocean-blue hair that fell in lazy, gorgeous waves over her shoulders. Her sea glass eyes saw everything. She was taller than me, but a childhood affliction had left her without use of her legs. I won't say she had a wheelchair. What she had was a custom-built throne rising above a single spinning orb, like the purest water supported her. I'd done my research and I still didn't understand how the thing worked, but I knew it was the driving purpose of her company. Much of the material she mined went straight to the seaside, where more marvelous chairs like hers were made.

As always, she wore a tailored suit, this one teal and cream. And as always, she made me feel like I was thirteen.

I fought the urge to hide my prosthetic hand behind my back.

"Leonine." Unlike most people in town, she used my full last name.

"Lark." I knew her full name, even knew her age—she wasn't any older than me. But I played it simple at first. "You know why I'm here?"

She set her elbows delicately on her desk, hands lifting and leaning into each other in a triangle. "I could guess."

"I'm not here for guesses." I took a step forward into the room.

"Good. We both have so little time to waste," she said, tilting her head as she smiled coolly.

I took another step, now on the plush rug. The office was sparse, but what it held was quality. Just like the tarot cards. "It's not like you to waste time with games."

"I would have thought the same of you."

"I'm here to end it," I said boldly, coming up to the desk. My hand was in my pocket.

"By all means," she agreed, reaching into a desk drawer. "Let's be done."

The threat was heady, but I nearly missed it. In the same moment that I'd thrown my three tarot cards down on the desk, Lark had thrown in two more.

* * *

In a small town like Belville, people like Lark stood out. They got things done. I'd learned a lot about her since I'd taken over the paper, and I'd be lying if I said our stories weren't similar. Coming from bigger cities, learning family trades, dealing with illness and accidents—and coming out stronger. Settling in a backwater with a plan to change things. I'd lost sight of mine, maybe, but I certainly wouldn't have ever planned to be standing in the mine headquarters bickering with Lark.

"My first one showed up on Valentine's Day," I said.

"I got *this* one at the new year," she shot back.

"The Hanging Man's more ominous than some—what is that? Adventurer?" I said.

"It's the *Fool,* and I personally find it an affront," she argued. "Not to mention just as ominous as some tied-up person, since it points to things unknown. But you'd know all about that, wouldn't you?"

"I don't know a thing about it," I confessed, nettled. "That's why I'm *here!*"

"Because some crook told you the silver on the cards was mine?" I'd given her the overview before we'd started pointing fingers. She'd been listening. Lark went on, "How do I know this isn't all part of your scheme to unsettle me?"

"Why would I want to unsettle you?" In the confusion, I'd forgotten to take any notes.

Lark slid her second card across the desk. While the first one was decorated with a person and a walking stick, labeled *0: the Fool*, this one depicted a woman with half-closed eyes and a ball of fire in one hand. *II: the High Priestess*, it read.

"Clearly you think I've become too powerful," said Lark. "You want me to lose my grip on my mine, on this mountain. You couldn't run me out with your articles and your politicking, so now instead—"

"What politicking? This is *Belville*," I retorted. "I haven't been trying to run you out. I don't care what you do."

"Then why have you been snooping through the mine's public records lately?"

"Because I thought *you* were the one sending me these," I said, frustrated. I waved at the Hanged Man, the Wheel, and the

Magician, which skittered across her polished desk as my hand pushed through the air.

Lark set her hands down on the desk, atop one another. She was always infuriatingly cool.

After a long, silent moment staring at me, she finally said, "Why would I send you tarot cards?"

I pulled up my cap and tugged at my hair. "I'm sure you'd breathe easier if I was gone."

"You *were* gone," Lark observed. "And then you came back."

"I left town on assignment, and that's all ancient history now," I said. "If you're trying to say that these cards are some holdover from that, don't bother."

"You have no idea where they're coming from," Lark concluded. "My, my. To have so many mysterious enemies that you can't trace a threat. What a life you lead!"

"You couldn't trace it either," I reminded her. "And that's with all of your staff at your command."

"My staff of miners," Lark corrected. I held her gaze. We both knew mining wasn't all that some of her staff did.

But then holding her gaze to prove a point became something else.

"Well," she said, finally. I hadn't moved, but I felt like I was falling. "We seem to be at an impasse."

"If you really want to stick to your story, that you didn't send these cards and neither you nor your staff know anything about them, then give me yours," I said. It was an impulse, but a good one. My reporter instincts rarely led me wrong. "I'll keep them all at the paper headquarters, and I'll use them to trace whoever *is* doing this."

Lark looked skeptical. "Why would having five of them help when three led you *here*?"

"Coming here was still a step forward," I declared. "Unless you think you'd find out more than me?"

"No, no," she said at last, with another cool smile. "You're the one who mines for secrets."

I ignored that. I'd published some stuff about her mining deals a few winters ago, sure, but everyone in Belville was fair game for a paper about Belville news.

"So tell me everything you know so far," I insisted. "And, moving forward . . ."

"Moving forward?" she echoed, still smiling at me.

"What I learn, I'll let you in on. And," I added, "if you get another card, you let me know."

* * *

Back in my office, I shuffled around the calendar board. With a little elbow grease and a *lot* of tearing down old notices, I soon had a usable cork board.

Up on the board went the Hanged Man, the Wheel, the Magician, the Fool, and the High Priestess.

I pinned up a few mining deals I'd found, too, as well as a few telegrams and newspaper clippings Lark had had her secretary give me.

When I stepped back and looked at it, though, something wasn't quite right. I decided to try shifting the cards around. I'd pinned them up in order of appearance. But they all had *numbers,* too.

The Wheel of Fortune and the Hanged Man, numbers ten and twelve. They went down on one end. Then Lark's cards—The Fool, zero, and the High Priestess, two.

I paused over the card I'd received that morning. The

Magician, one.

It was meant to go right between the cards Lark had received so far.

I wasn't quite sure what it meant yet, but as I stood back and looked at it, I could feel that spark. The spark of a new story, a new lead. Before we'd parted, Lark had made some jibe about the High Priestess card—it was fitting, she'd said, since reporters like me consider ourselves guardians of the truth. But I wasn't sure where the truth in this story was yet.

I *was* sure that I had the skill to find it, though.

I winked at the Magician card. In the spring light filtering through the windows, the little silver figure almost seemed to wink back.

* * *

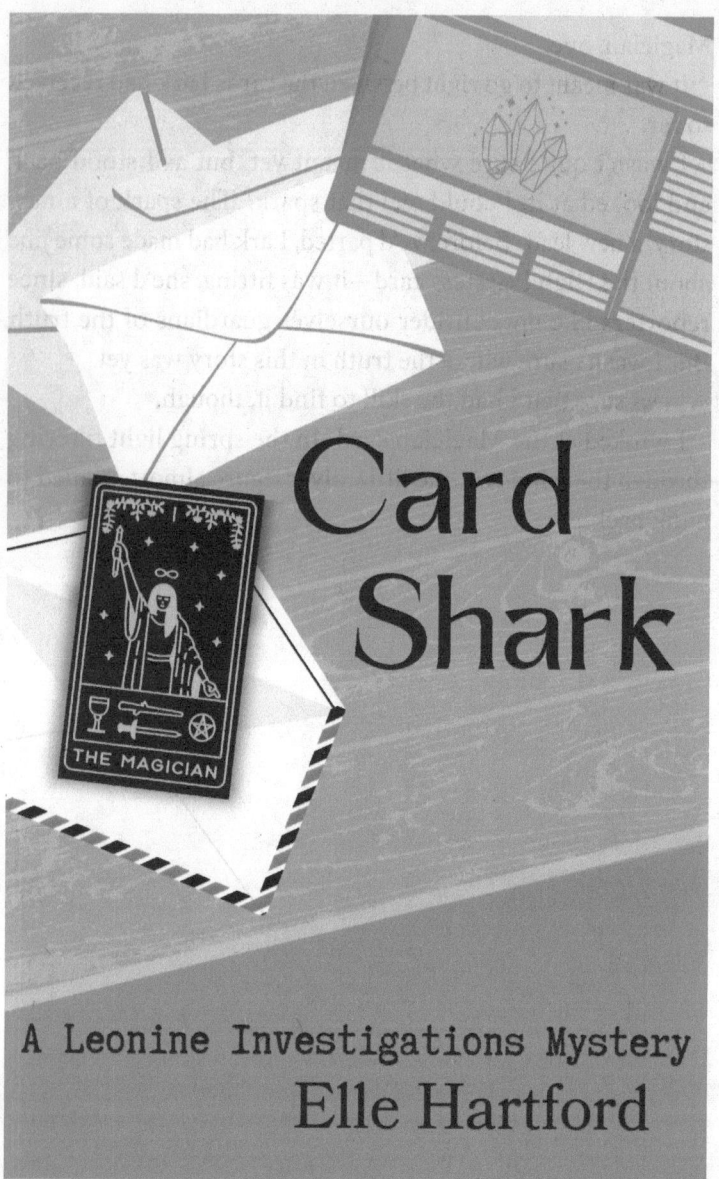

Card Shark

A Leonine Investigations Mystery
Elle Hartford

4

Close to the Chest

What kind of right does a little slip of paper have to ruin someone's day, anyway?

It was the end of the week and all I wanted was to put up my feet. This last newspaper had been a tough one. I'd had to run down two extra sources at the last minute for an expose on fowl-holding practices at the grocery stand, and one of my printing presses was on the fritz. It had been a scramble to get the final proofs ready. To say last night was a long one was an understatement.

But it was done. Now was the time to relax before the next round.

So of course, when I came back to newspaper headquarters after a long lunch, I found a white envelope sticking out of the mailbox by the back stairs.

I knew exactly what it was. I could feel the outline of the card through the thin envelope. As usual, there was no address, no handwriting, no stamp. No trace of how it had shown up. The game was getting tiring. Sure, it had led me to Lark last month, and that had been interesting. I still had the cards she'd received tacked up on my board, right next to mine. The Fool, the Magician, the High Priestess, the Wheel of Fortune, the Hanged Man. Three months since they'd begun appearing, and they had yet to tell a coherent story.

Was I curious about the next step? Sure. Any reporter would be. But I was tired. And when you're a one-woman show, you have to learn to pick your battles . . .

Below, the exterior door slammed. Heavy footsteps sounded as someone climbed the staircase up to the print shop. Nyx, the black cat that lived in the building, jumped up from her nap on top of a stack of paper on the shop floor. Sheets of newsprint tumbled through the air as she hissed and darted atop the cabinets that held the type.

The intruder knocked loudly at the shop door, but didn't pause. They were halfway through the rows of printing machines when I poked my head out of my office.

I could see the reason for the noise at once. My visitor was Skar, an oversized troll who worked at the mine. For Lark.

"Something wrong?" I asked him, ready to grab my hat and coat from the rack next to my office door.

"Nothing wrong," he returned, stooping so his head didn't hit the ceiling. "Delivery."

He held out an envelope. I could have invited him into the office, but his mining trousers and boots had already shed enough dirt on the shop floor. I might not have been the tidiest person, but that's why I decided to keep him where he was. I hated sweeping.

I took the envelope. It had the same stiff feeling of doom about it as mine had, but this one I opened.

And immediately closed. I cleared my throat. "Where'd you get this?"

34

"Lark got it," Skar said. "In the mail. But the post office says they know nothing."

"Today?" I asked.

"Today," the troll affirmed.

"Where is she?" I asked, trying to sound impartial.

Skar shrugged. "Fancy meeting this afternoon. Deal with a gem smith in New Dale. Lark has no time for errands."

Clearly he hadn't taken a peek at the card. I swallowed. "She's out of town?"

"Left this morning," said Skar. "Skaab went with her."

Skar turned to leave at this point. There was nothing more to say. Except—

"Wait," I said, as he reached the shop door. He glanced at me over one massive shoulder. I cleared my throat again. "Tell me the minute they get back."

"We'll send a pigeon," Skar said. He chuckled at his own joke as he lumbered down the stairs. The mine was a good half hour out of town, high on the mountain. Lark didn't like a lot of magic and spells mixed up in her business, so it was difficult to get word to or from the mine in good time. I didn't care.

The exterior door slammed below again. I raced back to my desk. In my haste to open my envelope, I ripped at its flap, giving myself a paper cut. That'd teach me for not using my prosthetic. But it didn't always respond as fast as I wanted it to.

The card that had been sent to me fell from my hands and skittered across my desk, face down. I lunged over to turn it right side up.

V: The Hierophant, it read. A silver etching of a scholar amongst stacks of books stared coldly up at me.

Creepy, maybe, but not so bad. I tossed the card intended for

Lark down on the table and looked at it again with a shudder. Against its black background, a silver snake slithered from the eye of an empty skull.

XIII was the number on hers. The label, *Death.*

* * *

Some words are only used by people trying to intimidate others. I'd met a few of the type as a reporter. So these days, I was prepared. In my office, several dictionaries took up space atop the filing cabinets full of past papers.

Hierophant: a person, often religious, who interprets sacred mysteries.

I knew nothing about the divine. I came from a line of reporters. No one in my family had ever used magic before. When I'd lost my right hand, we'd turned to technology rather than wishes and fairy gifts. Polished brass and clunking print machines and little notebooks scribbled with menial notes—that was my life.

But I knew exactly who'd have a different perspective.

I jammed my cap over the mess of auburn springs that passed for my hair and tightened my boots. I knew from my lunch break that it was unusually brisk in Belville for this time of year, but I didn't plan to be outside for very long. My dark canvas overalls and rolled-up shirtsleeves would be just fine. The last step: I tucked both cards gingerly into my notebook. Then I shoved the whole thing deep in a pocket and grabbed my keys on the way out the door.

Shadows chased me as I crossed the park. My print shop took up the second floor on a building at one end of Market Square, the heart of Belville. All I had to do was get to the other corner and duck into the café.

I paused as the front door swung shut behind me, panting like I'd run to the mine and back. The Pomegranate Café was full of diners. Clusters around tiny tables, lounging on the sofa under the front windows, chatting obliviously on the second floor balcony. Not one of them noticed me.

But Sakura did.

Her apron today was pastel peach collided with neon yellow. Somehow it managed to clash with everything, even with her white bob. Her pink spring dress didn't even stand a chance of matching. For a brief second I was glad she was behind a sales counter and a bank of magic coffee makers.

Magic. Sakura did nothing without it.

"Leo?" Her voice cut through the noise of her café. "Is something wrong?"

Just like Skar had, I shook the question off. I wove through the other customers until I'd reached the counter. "I need to go over something with you."

Her sharp blue eyes swept from my boots to my cap and back again. She met my gaze with a knowing smile. "Then you can do so over coffee and cake. Your usual?"

"I didn't come here for sugar and caffeine," I protested. "If you can't get Glacial to cover the counter, I'll come back—"

She interrupted me with a wave of her pale hand. "You came here because you need something, and that something includes a little boost. One moment, dear."

Without ringing me up, she turned to shout something through the café's kitchen door and then took a black coffee cup from the shelves lining the wall. Most of her china was colorful and floral. But she always gave me my order in that black cup.

I surrendered to the inevitability. I'm not the type to back down in a battle of wills, but Sakura's was legendary, and we were on her turf. Based on my research, she had to be at least half a dozen years my junior, but I let her shoo me toward a table in the back corner like I was a kid.

She sat with relish. With another wave of her fingers, she used sparkling black magic to float my coffee and a piece of dark chocolate torte over to our table, along with a tall pink mug that smelled like strong chai for herself. The saucers and silverware sailed through the air. Never once did they hit someone or spill a drop. In fifteen years of reporting, I'd met only one sorcerer who could have managed that kind of thing without preparation. *He* probably would have hit someone, maybe on purpose. This was beyond normal sorcery or Witch stuff. But it also wasn't showing off. It was just life as usual for Sakura.

And that's exactly why she'd topped my list for sacred magic practitioners.

When I pointed that out to her, though, she laughed at me. "If you want *sacred,* you'll have to talk to Hunter next time he comes through town. This is shadow magic, as you may recall from some of your more opinionated letters-to-editor."

I didn't think anyone actually *read* those. I rarely did. "Maybe shadow magic is better," I said, pulling my notebook from my pocket and setting it on the table. I couldn't quite remove my hand from it, though. It didn't seem right to just let it sit there. I leaned over it. "I've been getting these cards . . ."

"Your tarot cards." Sakura set her mug aside and nodded, satisfaction in her round face. "I was wondering when you'd come to ask me about them."

I was taken aback for only a second. That was how long it took to remember that I'd told William, one of the local gossips, about the Wheel card. No wonder Sakura'd heard all about it. "That saves us time," I decided, sliding the notebook across the table. "If you don't mind taking a look."

"Mind? Please." Sakura beamed as she drew the envelopes out and pulled the cards into one hand. When she saw the Death card, she didn't bat an eye. She moved her mug of chai aside with that same black magic and lay the Hierophant down first, so that the card faced me. "You said you got this today, and it made you think of me? I'm flattered. I think it looks more like Luca in his bookstore. And that's the first thing you have to understand about tarot: what the cards mean depends on *you*, the viewer. The way I interpret a card might not line up with the feeling you get from it."

"The other card looks pretty decisive," I said stiffly. I couldn't see the point in a bunch of divination cards if they could be interpreted in different ways.

Sakura smiled like she could read my thoughts. "The Death card. No need to be afraid of it, Leo."

"I'm not," I said, crossing my arms. "But it didn't come to me. That one went to Lark. She had it sent on to me because . . . we have an agreement."

"Oh, do you? That's cute." Sakura sipped innocently at her chai, like we weren't staring down a skull embossed on a calling card. "I know how it looks, love, but here's the second thing I can tell you about tarot: ninety-nine percent of the time, it is metaphorical. The Death card could mean the end of a job, a relationship, even a point of view. It's really more about a transformation, a change between phases. If you want my honest opinion, it's not even the most menacing card in the Major Arcana."

"Major Arcana?" I asked, my investigative instincts catching on the new phrase.

"That's the name for this specific group of cards," she said. "There's twenty-two Majors, and then the rest of the cards in a tarot deck are Minor Arcana. The Minors are usually less illustrative. By sticking with Majors, someone wanted to make sure you really got their point."

"I haven't," I grumbled. "Except Lark is in danger."

"Let's hold off on that assumption for a moment," Sakura suggested. "What other cards have you got so far?"

I checked my notebook and rattled off the list for her.

After listening intently, she nodded again. "Generally, the Major Arcana are thought to tell a story—starting with the Fool, progressing to the Magician, and so on. A cycle of life and rebirth. But someone is sending them to you very out of order, so they're probably not trying to remind you about the Hero's Journey."

"I don't need a refresher on literary devices," I agreed sourly.

"What you need is to eat your cake and drink your coffee before it gets cold," Sakura informed me. As I obeyed, she smiled again. "You've come to the right place to learn, but there's one more thing I have to tell you first. Tarot can only give suggestions—at the end of the day, the present and future depend on *you* and your actions. So. What are you aiming to do, Leo?"

* * *

The path up the mountain was tough, but I was tougher.

And I will admit that Sakura had been on to something when she made me eat that cake. Not only was it delicious, it fueled my hasty walk.

40

Sakura wanted to know my plan. The truth was, I didn't have one. Sometimes the best stories develop on their own—that's what my granda would say. I wasn't so sure about that myself, but I knew when I'd done things out of order. I could barely focus on what Sakura had to tell me. I should have gone up to the mine from the beginning.

It was late afternoon when I got to the mine's office building. The shadows from the forest were already long and deep like night. The mine itself, a gash in the mountain, was quiet. But work still bustled around the office building, which sat squarely in the middle of the sorting and loading area.

Skar opened the door for me. "But Lark's not back yet."

"Then I'll wait," I informed him. I took up residence at the empty desk in the front room. Maybe it'd do me some good to go over my notes about the tarot cards one more time. What was it Sakura had told me? I had written it down out of habit . . .

1. *Meaning of the card depends on the viewer*
2. *Cards' meaning is metaphorical*
3. *Cards don't actually predict the future*

Was that how she had put it? I scratched my head, tugging at my cap. That third point wasn't quite right. I didn't understand a thing about it. What use were these cards, anyway? Why bother sending them to me?

Sakura had mentioned action. Was someone trying to prompt me to act in a certain way?

The main door opened and closed. "I don't recall hiring a new secretary," Lark observed.

"You couldn't afford me." I said it on impulse. I regretted it when I looked at her. But at the same time, I was relieved. She looked exactly as she always did, her elf figure perfect and her tan skin glowing, aquamarine hair curling down in waves over the back of her wheelchair. Her face was shrewd and her gaze missed nothing. Behind her stood her actual secretary, a bland young man—classic bystander.

"If my luck continues as it did this afternoon, that might be true." Her chair hummed every so slightly as it skimmed across the floor, bringing her directly across from me. She might not like magic in her mine, but she used it to great effect in her products. I couldn't help but feel a little jealous.

And what had she said? What had *Sakura* said, about the Death card?

I cleared my throat. "What happened?"

"The deal is off." Lark didn't look too perturbed by it, but she also didn't make eye contact. Her sea green eyes were miles away.

"Did you look at the card you got today?" I asked.

That got her attention on me. "You think it's related?"

"If it is, it's not the worst that could have happened," I said without thinking. I showed her her card. *Death.* A dead deal was better than a dead person, even if it still wasn't good.

Lark watched me for a moment. "You were supposed to be investigating all this."

"I am," I promised. "I just learned something."

She smiled at that, just faintly, leaning her elbows on the table and steepling her hands. "Yes?"

"Yes," I said, leaning in. Confident. "Whoever is sending these isn't just doing it as a warning. They're trying to influence what *we* do."

"What we do in what arena?" Lark's delicate eyebrows

42

wrinkled. "In business? In the mine?"

I closed my notebook with a snap. "That's exactly what I'm going to find out next."

* * *

Close to the Chest

A Leonine Investigations Mystery
Elle Hartford

5

The Hand Dealt

When you're pinning things to the wall with thumbtacks and red string, you know you're in over your head.

That was fine by me, though.

You play with the cards you're dealt, my granda would say to me, *and as a reporter, you're playing an unknown game with a mystery dealer.*

Granda was the best of the best, the kind to uncover government cover-ups and mercantile plots. But he treated local gossip and kiddie fairs with the same seriousness. Whenever anyone in Belville asked about my family, I told them about Granda. Between you and me, I sometimes exaggerated the stories, throwing in lofty awards and death under cover. The truth was he was happily retired in the country.

But there was no need for busybodies in Belville to know that.

There *was* need, however, for me to get my facts straight. It had been four months now since some mysterious dealer took to sending me macabre cards. And not just me—Lark,

45

too, who was as close to "business mogul" as it came in Belville. I'd promised her last month that I'd figure out what the cards related to. I wasn't in the habit of making promises, and I sure wasn't about to break one.

Especially not when the most recent card to show up at Lark's door was a deathly skull. And right afterward, her new mining deal had gone six feet under.

On the cork board in my office at the newspaper headquarters, I had it all lined up. Seven cards stared down at me like black-and-silver mug shots. On the top row, the cards I had gotten so far: the Hanged Man, the Wheel of Fortune, the Magician, the Hierophant. On the row below, the cards sent to Lark: the Fool, the High Priestess. Death. With red string, I'd connected each card to a page torn out of my pocket notebook. On each page were the notes I'd collected. Sakura, local shadow witch, had been helpful in interpreting the cards—about as helpful as someone who says things like *in the end it's up to you, you know?* can be.

I'd also started pulling articles I'd written in *Belville & Beyond* for each of the past four months. If they seemed related to the cards, they went up on the board. Obviously my opinion piece about Lark's lost deal went up underneath Death. She hadn't been too pleased with that piece. I hadn't heard from her in a few weeks . . .

A knock on the newspaper door. I jumped. Lark's hench-trolls had incredible timing.

But they didn't come in when I yelled. I finally tossed my pile of back issues on my desk and crossed the shop floor myself. There was a path worn in the wood floor between the main door and my office. The printing presses were silent as I passed, and so was the black cat atop the shelves along the wall.

I yanked open the door, already talking. "Didn't you hear me? Why are you here? Did she get another card?"

But the person standing in the hallway was not a troll from Lark's mine. It was someone much smaller and more shifty-looking than that.

"Um, hello, sorry to bother you?" she said.

I squinted at her. She wasn't totally a stranger. But she *was* a relative newcomer in Belville. Slim, shrinking, hunched over. Worked at the hair salon, and according to rumor, had been seen leaving Officer Thorn's place at very early hours of the morning . . .

But what was her name?

"Um—were you expecting someone else?" she added.

She finally met my gaze. She had the air of someone who's made a play and might regret it. Taking in the silver hair and golden eyes, I recalled the rest. This was Magica, an ex-carnival acrobat who'd traded a shady past for idyllic domesticity and a career in hair care.

"I was," I told her flatly. "What did you come over for? Does Gloria want to run a new ad in the paper?"

"Um," said Magica, for the third time. "I don't know? Actually, that's not why I'm here. See, I guess, when Mel was doing her rounds, for the mail, I guess she accidentally took this envelope from your mailbox along with your outgoing mail, but she only realized it when she'd got as far as the salon, because we were asking her to check her bag for a payment that Gloria was expecting, but we didn't find it but we did find *your* letter, but Mel was super busy so . . . I said I'd bring it over?"

She was holding out a plain white envelope. During her entire speech. Waiting until the end to take it was excruciating. When I did take it, using my good hand, I could feel what it must be. I was an old hand at this game now.

I squinted at Magica again and made a decision. "You'd better come in for a minute."

* * *

VII: The Chariot, it read. A pair of wild horses pulling a cart ready to tip over at any moment was etched in silver on the black cardstock.

I sat at my desk and mused over the card for a moment. I made a point of ignoring Magica at first. She had her back to me, looking at my cork board mess. From behind my desk and piles of papers, I had some perspective. Magica was not the person sending me, or Lark, strange cards.

She *did* come across as the sort to leave anonymous letters rather than deal with someone face to face—that much was true. But not the sort who'd randomly give up leaving them in the mailbox to hand-deliver one, along with a flimsy story. And from the way her head was on one side as she looked at the cork board, she understood tarot even less than I did.

Besides, it wasn't unlike Mel to make a mistake. She'd made a very memorable one when she'd started out as Belville's postmistress. That time, it had ended with family coming in from New Dale and dramatic proposals in the Pomegranate Café. I made a mental note to pin my article about that drama up on the board as well.

At this rate, I'd take any connection I could get.

"She didn't know anything more about it?" I asked Magica.

"Mel? The letter?" Magica turned, her already wide eyes even wider. "I didn't think so. Should she have?"

"Did Gloria?" I pressed.

Magica shook her head, making her short hair wave in front of her tan face. "No, we all thought it was a little strange, since there was no name or anything. But Mel said you've gotten them before?"

"Who is 'we?'" I leaned across the desk.

"Um—me, and Gloria and Johann, at the salon." She walked over and collapsed into the one other chair in the office. "Did you have questions about it? Because I really don't know anything. Is it related to your board? Did you talk to Mina about it?"

Mina, a very familiar name for Officer Wilhelmina Thorn. I glanced at the Chariot on my desk, then up at her. "Why ask about the board?"

"It's—interesting?"

"Why suggest Thorn?"

"Um—she might help?"

I studied her. It did no good. Whatever she knew or didn't know about the tarot cards, Magica obviously had full faith in the local police force of one.

I did too, for that matter. But Officer Thorn and I had a very push-me-pull-you working relationship, and it wasn't worth the bother to involve her. Yet.

"What do you see?" I asked. "When you look at that board."

Magica glanced over her shoulder and the tarot cards and mess of string. "Um . . . I guess you're working on a big new story? It looks interesting. I think Saki reads tarot? I know Mina's worried about some of the changes at the mine, with them making new products. She said the same thing, like they were going down a strange path, like that first card on the bottom, that's what made me think of it."

The Fool. That's what had drawn her attention.

"I didn't say anything," I said, suspicious.

"Oh, but," said Magica, stumbling, "didn't you write all those articles?"

I looked back at the board. The bottom half was cluttered with snippets from back issues—the ones I'd gotten around to pinning up. Each one was related to the tarot cards . . . and each one was *about* the mine.

The answer had been staring me in the face. I'd been getting nowhere because I'd assumed that the cards had to do with *me*, maybe something I was doing in town. But they'd been about Lark and her mine all along. Someone was getting information about the mine *through my paper*.

* * *

I carted Magica along with me to the Pomegranate. We were listening to Sakura talk about Chariot cards and *forward movement* over coffee when I noticed a massive shadow headed for the hair salon.

It was bright summertime in Market Square, so I knew that shadow was out of place.

And it could only be one thing. One of Lark's trollish employees. Headed to see Gloria? Or had they been hoping to see Magica for some reason? No, the troll came and went from the salon, and all the while Magica sat next to me with her rapt gaze on Sakura.

But what business did Lark have with the salon?

I decided I'd heard enough about *action*. It was time for real movement. I left Magica and Sakura chatting and took the path to the mine at a brisk walk. The shade of the forest was a relief. But it didn't make me feel better. Officer Thorn—via

50

Magica—had been right. It wasn't just the new mine deal last month. Lark had been branching into all kinds of new mineral refinement, ever since the new year. I couldn't believe it had taken me so long to make the connection.

When I reached the mine office, I breezed right past the secretary. With cards meaning things like *endings* and *movement* on the table, we'd lost the time for niceties.

But when I opened with my salon question, Lark laughed at me.

She sat behind her large desk, enthroned as ever in a wheelchair so finely crafted it made my printing presses and prosthetics look like child's play. I always had a hard time looking away from Lark. But today, her beachy blue hair was especially wavy, her sand-colored fingers especially polished, her aquamarine eyes especially arresting.

"You should try having business of your own at the salon some time," she said.

I tugged my cap lower over the wild springs that passed for my hair. Privately, I doubted even Magica and Gloria could do anything for my appearance. A manicure wouldn't fix the ink stains on my fingers and it wouldn't make me better at my work, either.

"That's all this is?" I insisted.

Lark waved one perfect hand. "Gloria came up yesterday. I didn't have her full fee on hand, so I sent it down today. Why? Are you jealous?"

"I'm worried about a different kind of mail."

"I'm not worried about *any* kind of person, myself."

"This isn't the time for jokes. I meant—"

"I know what you meant," Lark said, her face becoming resolute. "And I won't hear it. I'm tired of people attempting to dictate my choices."

"You got a card," I inferred.

My interrogations might have gotten me nowhere with Magica, but I knew Lark. I knew when she was being coy about something—and she knew I knew it.

"Yesterday," she admitted. With distaste, she opened a drawer and pulled out a single black card, flicking it so it skimmed across the desk to land in front of me.

I stood with my hands on my hips at first, just looking at it. *IX: The Hermit*, this one said. A lone figure held a lantern that illuminated nothing but its own face. All it looked like to me was a softer version of Death.

"This is why," Lark said, looking at me with pursed lips. "Before you ask. *This* is why I didn't send it on to you. Because I knew exactly what you'd say."

"*I* don't even know what I'm going to say," I retorted. "What will get through to you? This is serious!"

"Yes, thank you, you said that last time," Lark shot back. "But as I've just told *you*, I refuse to follow orders from some recluse card dealer."

"The mining itself is what this has been about all along," I blurted out.

"All the more reason that *no one* can tell me what to do with my business," said Lark, lifting her chin.

I began pacing to and fro along the desk. "You've already lost one big deal."

"And you did seem *so* sad about that in the papers," she said dryly. "So I expect you to be happy for me when I tell you that I have found my own way forward."

"Prompted, no doubt, by a cursed card that *obviously* means you should keep to yourself and let it alone!"

"Prompted by no one but myself," Lark corrected. "I was already going to do it. Now I'm simply going to do it with extra style. You can scowl at me all you like, Leonine, but I am moving forward. Soon, my new stores of mesmerized silver will be available to anyone in Beyond."

I stopped and stared her down—even though I knew it was no use. She wouldn't cave. The cards were pointing one direction, and Lark was determined to go the other.

In that moment I knew exactly what it was like to drive a cart pulled by wild horses.

But it didn't matter. I was being pulled against my will, sure, but I also had my best lead yet.

I stormed out of Lark's office . . . to learn everything I could about mesmerized silver.

* * *

The Hand Dealt

A Leonine Investigations Mystery

Elle Hartford

6

Courting Cards

There's one problem with anyone who promises to have all the answers you need.

They're sure to disappear the moment you need them.

It had been a full month since I started on the mesmerized silver lead. I knew that mining magnate Lark was making deals to sell it, and I knew that some mysterious tarot card-sending creep didn't like that. But I had to figure out why any of it mattered. Or what mesmerized silver was in the first place.

Lark wasn't telling. She was keeping her business practices close to the chest, and I couldn't blame her. We may have been cooperating over the tarot cards, but we'd had our unpleasant run-ins about her decisions in the past. And no one who's come up with a secret magical process would run to tell the paper about it.

Is that all she thought of me as? The hard-headed reporter and owner of *Belville & Beyond*?

No need to dwell on it, I told myself. What I needed to dwell on was this bloody ore. That's bloody in a figurative sense, of course. Not literal. Not yet . . .

But right when I needed her, the one expert who could help skipped town to visit her family. I'd never heard of an alchemist taking a holiday before, especially one with such perfect timing. But the fact remained that Red was gone and one of her minions was running Red's Alchemy & Potions in her stead. The last thing I needed was more dealings with minions.

Unless they were *my* minions.

I'd hired some part-time research assistance. Belville being the backwater that it is, I couldn't find any retired PIs or up-and-coming reporters eager to prove themselves. I wouldn't have trusted them anyway. Instead, I hired Magica, from the salon. She'd already gotten involved in the tarot affair, and she knew enough that it was best to keep her close.

She also made a point of bringing me a coffee every time she came into the office.

"Large, iced, extra black." She announced herself this way every week, walking into the print shop and then to the door of my office with a little more confidence each time. This time, she even made it over the threshold before pausing for me to say something.

"Thanks, Magica." When I sat up and pulled my feet off the desk, a cascade of old papers followed. I tossed my battered *Encyclopedia Mineralia* in the empty spot. "You can leave it here."

She crossed the office floor gingerly. The worn wood boards were hidden under piles of research and a couple baskets of sunflower seed packets leftover from the town's solstice festival. The cork board still boasted a line of tarot cards and red string connecting each one to related articles. In the gloom, her shoulder-length silver hair was a bright reminder of everything

I hadn't discovered yet.

"I told you, you could call me Maggie. Everyone else does." She set the ceramic to-go container on a mostly-clean patch of desk.

I nodded, tugging at my cap as I settled in to read another article.

But she didn't leave. Normally she worked at a makeshift desk atop a broken printing press on the shop floor. Today she hesitated, looking at the cork board.

I sighed, letting my article fall back against the edge of the desk. "What is it?"

"I was just thinking. Isn't it about time . . ."

"Time for what?"

"Time for . . ." She gestured vaguely.

I frowned. "I already told you, I clean when I'm between projects. If it bothers you, then you can go—"

"That's not what I meant," Magica said hurriedly. "It's just, looking at your board, isn't it time for another tarot card to show up?"

"Oh. That." I glanced at the lineup too. "Nyx has it."

Magica's golden eyes drifted up. I knew exactly what she'd see. On the old shelf high above my head, a winged black cat was sitting with her front paws atop a plain white envelope.

"If you think you can get it from her, be my guest," I added. Then, in a whisper, I confessed, ". . . I'm too short to reach it."

* * *

It took two minutes. Magica coaxed Nyx down from the shelf with pet phrases and promises of the whipped cream off the top of her mocha.

The traitorous cat picked up her booty and soared down to the shop floor like it had been her plan all along.

Magica and I followed Nyx out into the shop. Nyx often perched on the cabinets that lined one wall, but this time she settled on one of the printing machines in the middle of the room. While Magica shifted whipped cream to her drink's lid, I snatched the envelope from the distracted cat.

One of the nice things about having a prosthetic hand is that you're immune to cat swipes. In that one hand, anyway. Nyx hissed at me, but I wasn't paying attention. Fact was, she had stolen two envelopes, not just one.

Magica looked over when I didn't say anything. "Oh! Has that ever happened before? How'd she get two?"

"She stole *all* my mail this morning. It's her new obsession," I said, sparing a glare for the cat. The cat ignored me. "This was the only thing in the mailbox. But it looks like Lark forwarded hers on too. See?"

I showed Magica the second envelope, which was stamped *sent on from the office of Lark* with an official air.

"That saves time, then," Magica said.

"Sure." It also saved me a chance to go in person and convince Lark to tell me everything she was holding back. I wasn't too happy about the missed opportunity.

I set my feelings aside, though, and opened the envelopes one after another. From mine, a familiar black card emerged. This time, the silver-etched picture was of a man with a crown and a stern expression. *IV: The Emperor,* it said.

"Yeugh." I tossed the card to Magica and focused on Lark's card. It was eerily similar, but instead of a man, it depicted a woman reclining on a throne above the words *III: The Empress*.

"What's wrong with this one?" Magica looked at the Emperor

first, then glanced at the Empress when I held it up. "That one doesn't seem so bad either," she added.

"It's the right one for Lark," I agreed dryly. "But I don't like it. It means whoever's sending these still knows a lot more than we do. Haven't you ever heard that pride comes before the fall?"

"I guess so." Magica looked down at the Emperor in her hand again, tilting it back and forth as the silver shone against the black.

"As for that one, I just don't like him," I declared. "He's too smug. He looks like he's too used to getting everything his own way in his domain."

The silence lasted just a little too long.

Both Magica and Nyx were staring at me.

"What?" I crossed my arms.

Magica glanced at the cat and chuckled. "Well, if you think about it . . . the newspaper kind of *is* your empire."

"Of course it's mine," I retorted. "But that doesn't mean I'm some kind of tyrant."

Nyx flicked her tail with a disagreeable air.

"Anyway," I said, "I don't see the point in comparing me to a king. What's that have to do with the ore? I don't have any of it."

"But you have all this," Magica said, gesturing at the print shop. "And all your leads. Maybe . . . it means you're on the right track?"

Leads? I had one lead, and it was looking like a dead end. The closest I'd been to silver in the past few weeks was this cursed tarot card.

I tossed the card down and strode over to the windows. They lined one wall of the shop, looking out from the second floor over Belville's heart, Market Square. From there, I could look down on kids playing and merchants selling and couples meandering through the park with their coffees . . . And know that every single one of them was hiding something.

And me? I was hiding two things: how worried I was that we were headed for disaster, and how frustrated I was that I couldn't see it coming.

Carts rattled down the road below. They passed right under my window, heading south toward the lake. It wasn't unusual to see these shipments of ore coming down from the mine on the mountain. Each cart was packed full and covered with a canvas tarp, pulled by a stone horse.

You read that right. Stone horses, another of Lark's little *pet* projects. Actual work horses are rare in Beyond. Hard to force an animal to work when most animals are magical or at least sentient. So instead, Lark had her miners gather up the scrap stone and then hired some fancy sorcerer to create these literal forces of nature. Huge and strong, each horse moved like an earthquake, the lumps of gray stone bunching and sliding like muscles.

Is it any wonder I was worried what she might have planned for magical silver ore?

Yes—Lark owned her empire. Even if that empire could get her into trouble.

I watched the carts go by, one by one, bound for the world outside of Belville. Except one.

One cart at the end of the line. Its driver was more slight than the other drivers, his wide-brimmed hat pulled low over his head against the summer sun. I couldn't see anything else about him, but my instinct was on point. Something did happen. His front wheel snapped just as he hit the end of Market Square.

60

His horse ground to a halt. I could see the driver waving to the others ahead: *go on, I'll catch up.* I almost felt bad for him.

But then, as soon as they were out of view, he waved that hand in a different direction. With a snap of his fingers, his front wheel flew back into place. He pulled the horse in a different direction and the cart started to trundle past the tavern.

With a broken wheel? Not possible. But he was going, and fast.

Good thing I knew every single street in Belville like the back of my hand.

"Change of plans," I called to Magica. I whirled on my heel. For some reason—call it more instinct—I grabbed both tarot cards on my way toward the door. I was already running. "I have a cart to catch!"

I could hear Magica's feet on the stairs behind me. In a flash of black, I saw Nyx swoop out the door above me. But I was focused on my prize. I dashed into the alley and hung a left, sprinting toward Market Square and the lost cart.

The first sprint was easy. He'd gone straight down the road at the bottom of the Square, and chasing down interviews in the past had been good exercise. I ran past the tavern and shops into shadow. At a corner I skidded to a halt, but not fast enough.

He was right there, to my left. The cart was pulled over to the side of the road, the driver looking back over his stock. I had no time. He saw me at once. And with my wild, wind-blown hair and panting breath, there wasn't any mistaking that I'd run after him. He snarled at me, and I grinned back, pulling out my notebook.

But then he lifted a crossbow to his shoulder.

Before he could shoot, a black shape darted out of the sky.

Nyx dove and then rose again, clutching strips of his hat in her front paws. The driver was irate. His crossbow was knocked aside and forgotten. He spat some curses but wasted no more time in driving off.

I took off after him again.

He took a corner on two wheels, trying to lose me on the narrow residential roads. I could have told him he never had a chance. I vaulted over a fence through a yard and caught up at the next intersection, so close I could almost leap into the back of the cart. Before my hand made contact, though, he spurred the horse down another alley, this time knocking over a rain barrel in his wake.

I had no choice but to run through the water. Fortunately I was in my boots. I didn't slip, but the dirt road was now mud, and it slowed me down. I made it to the corner, breathless, just in time to see him rattle down the road into the forest.

Nyx swooped overhead. I slowed, shaking my head. It was no use following an outlaw into the forest. Desperate as I may have been, I was not stupid. I knew to stick to my own domain.

As I caught my breath I glanced down. Clutched in my hand were those two tarot cards, still. Light flashed off the silver like the Emperor was winking at me. In that moment I made my decision.

"Who was it? Was it something to do with the cards?" Magica called as she caught up with me.

I turned to look at her. She was more fit than I was, hardly out of breath. But still, what had she expected to do when confronted with a crossbow and an angry miner with his rock horse? Why had she come along?

Come to think of it—why had Nyx come along? Usually the cat acted like she was royalty and I was dirt.

But today, Nyx settled on to my shoulder.

I looked again at my assistant.

"Maggie," I said, firmly, "I don't know yet. We might not have answers now, but we'll get them. Let's get back to the shop. If the paper is my empire, then I'll use that to flush them out."

* * *

Courting Cards

A Leonine Investigations Mystery

Elle Hartford

7

Tipping the Hand

I'm always happy when I'm on the hunt.

In fact I was pretty pleased with myself as summer wore on. The weekly series on "Misbehavior in the Mines" was going well. Each article had featured a particular company or policy that was unsavory, and they'd all been satisfying to write.

If some miner wanted to send me threatening cards and thought I'd play it straight, they were about to learn otherwise.

That's if they hadn't learned their lesson already. I'd published four articles so far and hadn't heard a peep. Aside from general reactions from the common folk, of course. My paper may have been just the local rag for Belville, but it was shipped to several nearby cities. I *knew* my stories were getting eyes on them. And for once, the monthly tarot card delivery was late.

It felt like victory. I should have known it wouldn't last.

But in the moment, life wasn't bad. I sat in my office with my boots on the desk. Nyx, the black raven-winged cat, had perched on a shelf within reach for once. I was petting her, listening to the summer storm out the window and getting a bit of rest in before gearing up to print the next edition of the paper, when my assistant barged in.

"Leo," she cried, "I just checked the mail on my way up."

Normally the letters that arrived at the paper headquarters were nothing to get excited about. Requests for ads, opinion pieces, junk. I could only think of one reason to get worked up over any of it. I sat up.

Nyx startled and flew out of the office onto the shop floor, her wing knocking my cork board of mining details and tarot cards askew on the wall. I tugged my cap to make sure it was covering the frizzy, distracting mess that counted as my hair. Then I cleared my throat. "So?"

"Um." After her first announcement, Maggie hesitated. Maggie made a great assistant—she was so good with organizing the back issues and reaching out to advertisers that I'd considered bumping her up to more than one day a week. But if something worried her, she had a hard time spitting it out. "One of them was addressed as a letter to the editor, uh, and we had talked about me doing those since you're working on the expose on giant abuse at the Southwell Mine, um, so I—I did open that one, before I came up, and—" Her voice trailed off, her pale arms wrapped around a stack of mail. She looked even shorter and slighter than usual, though her golden eyes were huge.

"You didn't find the cards?" I asked. I'll admit I was confused.

"Oh—I did," she said, shaking short silver hair back. "Here, I found this one for you, and one I think was forwarded on from Lark's office."

She shuffled in her pile of mail and threw two plain, unstamped envelopes onto my desk. On one, Lark's secretary had scribbled a note to the postmaster requesting it be sent on to me. Lark and I had kept to this arrangement for months now. We both got the tarot cards, but I was the one researching them.

Lark had her mine to focus on . . . a mine I hadn't covered in one of my exposés. Yet.

As Maggie watched, I emptied the cards onto the table. As usual, there were no notes. From my envelope, a black shiny card with silver engraving depicting a shining sun plopped out. *XIX: The Sun,* it read. That was straightforward enough. Lark's card showed a silver moon nearly hidden by clouds, labeled *XVIII: The Moon.* If I didn't know better, I would have thought they were a matched pair.

"Um—did you know they would come today?" Maggie asked.

I was busy tapping one of the cards on the table. Just as solid as ever. And there for a moment I'd thought I was free of them somehow . . . "What?"

"How did you know? That they were in the mailbox?"

"They'd hardly be in the chimney, would they?" I regretted the quip instantly. It reminded me that Nyx had once lived atop the print shop roof and caused all kinds of trouble. Cards in the mailbox were just fine in comparison, thanks very much. "Anyway, I didn't know. No idea. Wait," I realized. "If you weren't worked up about the cards, then what was it?"

"Um, it was this," Maggie said, waving a large tan envelope. "I think you'd better read it."

* * *

A whole day later and I still couldn't *stop* reading it.

Miss Mary Jane Leonine . . .

Coward. Made a point of using my whole name and didn't even bother signing a real one to the letter.

. . . hereby inform you that your publication, "Belville & Beyond" . . .

67

My "publication!" Like I hadn't poured my adult life and experience into this paper.

. . . citing certain recent articles on the mining industry . . .

That part did make me smile.

. . . charged, in cooperation with the Police Guild, to cease and desist with these malignant rumors or prepare to pay for related business damages.

They were trying to shut me down. Me!

Since the tarot cards began appearing, there had been real life consequences. Lark had lost a deal at her mine, and had a cartload of ore stolen. But that was mining nonsense. It was infighting and unprofessional competition, the way I saw it. It wasn't anything to do with my pursuit of the *truth*.

Folks rely on the newspaper to tell them the truth when everyone else wants to cover it up. That's what my Granda used to say to me.

Now it was clear that someone wanted to cover my story up.

When Maggie offered to set up a meeting with the local police, I had my doubts at first. I hadn't done anything wrong. I wasn't about to troop down to the station like a criminal. But then she suggested meeting at the local café, and she promised to be on hand in case things took a turn. That made me feel better. She'd never admit it, but Maggie had sway with the police in town.

Because the total police presence in Belville was one lone officer. And Maggie was dating her.

I ordered my usual at the counter, extra black. I had the letter and the tarot cards in one arm. There hadn't been any reason to bring the cards, but I couldn't help myself these days. They were like weird little talismans. I couldn't tell if they were reassuring or terrifying.

The first tarot cards to arrive had been things like The Hanged Man and Death. But this Sun and Moon business . . . what *was* that?

"New delivery?" the café owner asked.

At first I startled. I thought for a moment she'd been staring at my right arm, a burnished copper prosthetic from the elbow down. But Sakura knew better. She was a shadow witch with a few old wounds and secrets herself.

"Not for you," I said, regaining my cool as I realized she was talking about the tarot cards I'd been tapping on the counter again.

"Too bad," she said with a cheeky grin. "The Sun's usually considered a good omen, you know—someone shining, in their prime. Though I like the Moon better as a card . . . it's more about secrets and mystery."

"You offering free advice with your coffee these days?" Truthfully, I appreciated her insight. I was already committing it to memory so that I could write it down in my notebook once I reached the table with Maggie and Officer Thorn.

Sakura winked across the counter. "Only to my favorite customers."

* * *

A few moments later, willing myself to be calm, I sat at a table set under the front window of the Pomegranate Café. The sun was shining hard on the wet trees in the Square. Outlined by the light, Maggie sat next to her hulking girlfriend, Officer Thorn.

Thorn and I had had our run-ins, of course. As Police Guild graduates went, she was a good one—not that I'd say that to her face. It's always best to keep officials on their toes. In her blue uniform and her perfectly styled long black hair, Thorn embodied "official." The broad shoulders, green orcish skin, and bullhorn-like voice helped too.

"Maggie says you're having trouble," the officer said over her extra-large chai. She'd lowered her voice a little. The entire two-story café *almost* didn't hear.

"I'm not having trouble," I said quietly. I passed the large envelope over the table. "I had a threat, that's all."

Officer Thorn glanced over the document and whistled. "That's a sight more threatening than those cards you were asking about, I'd say."

"I've had more of those too," I admitted. "I believe they're related."

"Got any reason to think so?" Thorn's brown-eyed gaze on me was keen.

I couldn't quite put my instincts into words.

But then Maggie leaned in. "The tarot cards are the whole reason she wrote those specific articles in the first place," she told Thorn. "Right, Leo?"

"I would have got to those stories eventually," I said, "but the tarot business made it pressing, if you know what I mean."

"I did wonder about the new series. I figured business around town must be slow," Thorn said. Before I could protest the slight, she added thoughtfully, "What were you planning to do about this?"

I hid my irritation behind a sip of coffee. "Figure out who sent it. Then go at them with all I've got."

"In other words, take matters into your own hands?" Officer Thorn's face was carefully blank.

"You can't," Maggie said, leaning in with much more emotion.

"Leo, don't do that. If they've already involved the Police Guild on their end, then you could wind up in a lot of trouble! Mina, tell her."

"I don't need her to tell me," I said, frowning. "This isn't the first time someone's been upset with my reporting."

But those times, I had been working freelance.

This was the first time *Belville & Beyond* was at risk. If I was legally bound to pay damages, and they cost more than my meager savings, then my paper would be the next domino to fall . . .

And for as much as I might complain about small town Belville, I wouldn't risk my paper.

The potential cost was blinding.

My inner conflict must have shown on my face. Officer Thorn sounded sympathetic when she spoke. "The seal is there, so someone in the Guild *is* already involved. Based on the return address, the complaint must have been filed in New Dale. I can poke around and see who will talk to me there."

I sat up. "And if they tell you who—"

"I'll poke around *if* you promise not to 'go at' anyone involved," Officer Thorn said, interrupting me. "Think about it. You've already tipped your hand. This is probably the response they want from you."

I hated to admit it. But she had a point. In writing my articles, I'd already revealed how much I knew and how exactly I aimed to take down bad business practices. That was the point of putting the truth out there.

And sometimes, I thought, with a silent apology to Granda, the truth couldn't stand on its own.

"I'll promise," I said. It pained me. "But since I'm playing along, what's the procedure?"

71

"When a warning like this is sent, you have options," Officer Thorn said. She considered the letter on the table. "First is you can stop writing about them altogether. There's not a judge or officer mentioned here, which means they're not currently planning on showing up in court. Not unless you keep writing about them, anyway. If you do keep writing and they have a case, then you'll get another letter or visit from an officer and you'll have to go to court to settle the grievance. You *could* try to settle the matter personally."

"But if they're already willing to talk to the police then maybe you shouldn't," Maggie added.

I agreed. Whoever had sent this was *not* trustworthy.

"You could take a gamble as to whether they can prove their claim or not," Officer Thorn said. "There's a chance the judge would rule you were just doing your job as a reporter. But if this is one of those mining operations filing against you, they'll have money and time to make their argument. And given that they're in New Dale . . ." She shook her head. "I've heard conflicting things."

That could only mean one thing. *Corruption.* The justice system in Beyond, maintained by the Police Guild and courts, relied on magical constraints and honorable rules to keep corruption from its ranks—on the whole. But every once in a while, there were cracks where the shadow crept in.

"So for now, I'll tell you what *I'd* say the procedure should be," Officer Thorn said with a small, crooked grin. "Let me deal with this as a professional. And you stick to your profession. Get all the facts you can. Just maybe don't put them in the paper yet."

Just *sit* on all the stories I'd yet to publish? I couldn't help but remember what Sakura had said. *Someone in their prime.*

I'd been feeling at the top of my game—but then I'd gone and tipped my hand. I knew Officer Thorn had proposed a valid plan.

But still, I couldn't help but wonder where Lark was, in all of this. Did she know about this latest move?

Perhaps it was time for another trip up to the mine.

* * *

Tipping the Hand

A Leonine Investigations Mystery

Elle Hartford

8

Card Reader

When you're after a story, the time to take a risk is yesterday.

That's what my granda would say.

I was itching to take his advice. There was a fall breeze tapping at the windows of the print shop, and the trees in Market Square were starting to go golden. This tarot harassment had gone on too long.

Nyx the raven-winged black cat was snoring atop one of the printing presses nearby. I'd sent my assistant, Maggie, home early. She'd turned my office into a mess of red string and old articles. The tarot cards that had come through the mail, two or more each month, were lined up on the cork board like a firing squad.

And that's why I'd chosen to pace the shop floor instead.

It was time to clock out—past time, actually. But can a reporter ever truly "clock out?" My granda never could. Maybe that's why he was one of the best.

Me, I couldn't even make sense of a bunch of sociopathic greeting cards . . .

But greeting cards would have been easier, because they come in more variety. The choices people made were clues. I knew this. Here's what was eating me: the choices that my strange correspondent *hadn't* made. Every card sent so far had been one of the Major Arcana, which Maggie assured me were the twenty-two most important cards in a tarot deck. They certainly had been suggestive. But with thirteen cards sent so far—either to me or to my associate, Lark, the owner of a local mine—the remaining choices were whittled down. Only nine possible cards left.

And some of those cards looked nasty.

Maggie had pulled up a list to compare our cards against. So far, receiving cards like the Hermit and the Hanged Man had heralded lost business deals, theft, and intimidation. With remaining cards named things like "The Devil" and "Judgment," I had to wonder what more I was in for.

And it wasn't just me—there was Lark to think of, too.

Nyx swatted at me as I passed by her printing press.

"Not now," I said.

Nyx mewed.

"Fine," I said.

Witty debate over, I set my troubles aside and went to get dinner for the cat.

* * *

It wasn't yesterday, it was *tomorrow*—another day at the paper, and I hadn't come up with a plan.

There was the latest edition of *Belville & Beyond* to put out, but I didn't have the heart to work on it. I paused in the door to my office, my long coat and newsboy cap still on. Everything was quiet. Not even Nyx was in—she must have wormed her way outside to bathe in the last of summer's sun.

Fine.

I turned on one heel and went back out the door, down the stairs and into the alley. Something hot and caffeinated, that's what I needed. I walked across the Square to the Pomegranate Café.

It was too late for the early regulars, and too early yet for everyone else. The café was quiet as I stepped inside. Behind the counter, there was a stranger.

She had lavender hair, pulled back in pigtails. Her skin was pale blue, a fact made more obvious by the smudge of flour on her cheek. There was more flour powdered across her pink apron. Despite her pastel appearance, she regarded me without friendliness.

"Your order?" she asked finally.

"Do I look like I have things in order?" I retorted. Exasperated, I pulled off my cap with my good hand and tugged my fingers through my wild hair. This letter business had made me even *more* suspicious than usual. Everyone looked like they might make a hobby of sending enigmatic warnings.

"Looks can be deceiving," she said.

Philosophy. That was unexpected. I had figured she was just impatient. Looking her over again, I noticed the businesslike way her sleeves had been rolled up—and the scars revealed underneath.

I almost pulled out my notebook. There had to be a story there. "Who are you?"

The stranger grimaced. "It's my café as much as Saki's."

"And where *is* Saki?"

"On her break. We may not have order, but we do have a

77

schedule."

Despite myself, I cracked. With a chuckle, I let my shoulders relax. "You must be the baker."

"Glacial," she said, agreeing with me. "Do you know what you want yet?"

I sighed. "Give me the darkest roast you have. Straight. Black. In the biggest mug you can find."

Glacial shrugged and rang me up.

But when she brought my coffee out to my table, there was a small orange macaron on the saucer beside it.

I'd taken over one of the couches beside the front left window. Why not—there wasn't anyone else in the café, except for a few dedicated tea drinkers on the second floor balcony. And, after a moment, another person who came out to join me: the missing Sakura.

She plopped herself on the couch across from me without preamble. "I heard you were trying to scare Glacial," she said. "Did it work?"

I raised an eyebrow. "Does it ever?"

"I've only ever seen one person manage it," Sakura said with a grin. She was fond of poofy skirts and matching hats—today's ensemble was in an autumnal maroon and gold. Her sleek white bob was tucked behind her ears, making her blue eyes look even bigger. Much like her baker who seemed ready to fight, she was a café owner intimately acquainted with dark magic.

And she'd helped me out with the tarot affair more than once, so I didn't mind admitting, "I didn't mean to take out my frustration on her. I guess I was looking for you. Those cards have me worked up."

"Tarot only pulls out of you the things that are already there,"

Saki said in a singsong voice. "How many times have I told you that now?"

"What about the cards that aren't here yet?" I asked, leaning in. I drew my notebook from my pocket and showed her the list that Maggie had made—the list of cards we hadn't yet received.

"Ooh, the Lovers, won't that be fun," she said, grinning coquettishly as she read from the list.

"I'm more concerned about *Judgment*," I retorted.

"Yes," said Saki, more soberly, "I can imagine so—especially after the legal action of last month. Has anything more come of that?"

"Not yet," I said. It was true—I hadn't heard another word from my would-be persecutor. But it was *killing* me to sit back and let Officer Thorn look into the matter, as I'd promised.

"I imagine Maggie is making sure you stay in line," Saki said. She wore that knowing look she often had. As someone who ferreted out information for a living, I could respect her insight. She went on, "You haven't had any new cards yet?"

"Not yet," I confirmed again.

"The look on your face could sour milk," Sakura declared, clearly amused. "Well, don't worry, dear. I'm sure they'll come. In fact—isn't there someone at the window for you now?"

I turned, bewildered. But it wasn't a henchman or a law officer.

It was Nyx . . . and she had two envelopes dangling from her fanged mouth.

* * *

I brought the envelopes into the café to deal with. After all, I wasn't done with my coffee. Nyx flew off, but Sakura remained, leaning over the table to study the cards as I tossed them down.

"That's the first time they've come by flying cat, I take it?" she asked.

"It's not Nyx who brings them," I said, though I *had* suspected the cat in the very beginning. "They come to the print shop mailbox. Nyx probably found them there and figured she was doing me a favor by hunting me down. Who knows how cats think?"

"Who indeed," Saki agreed.

"That one was to me," I went on, handing over a black card embossed with the silver letters *XVII: The Star* and an ominous illustration of a star over a pool. "Nothing else in the envelope, as usual. And this one—Lark has her secretary forward hers on to me. There's his note on it, but nothing else. And—" I pulled out the card and stopped speaking. For a moment, my heart was in my throat.

XX: Judgment, it read. The silver illustration depicted a large fire with a phoenix rising from it.

I handed the card to Sakura.

"It's simple, but still a very dramatic deck," she observed. "They really convey a lot with just line drawings, don't they? It's rather clever."

"Clever?" I nearly choked on the word. "It's malicious!"

"Oh, my dear. Judgment can be a bit . . . *monumental,* I'll give you that," said Sakura. "But the Star is usually more of a sign of destiny or hope. A positive rebirth. And the rebirth in Judgment can be positive too, if you make the right choices."

"The *right choices!*" I repeated, outraged. "According to whom? No doubt the card sender thinks the 'right choice' is just to give everything up—stop writing about the mining industry, and stop whatever deal Lark is making. They'd like nothing better than to think they cowed us into silence!"

"Actually," Sakura said thoughtfully, "I think you've just made an excellent reading."

"A what?"

"A reading," she repeated, patient. "It means looking at the cards and drawing conclusions. When you first came here to ask me about tarot, you wanted *me* to make conclusions for you. But by now, you've learned enough to interpret your messages on your own."

I wasn't sure I'd take *that* much credit. But I did see the value in this breakthrough. Until this point, I'd been completely in the dark about what the card sender *wanted*. Sure, there'd been that "cease and desist" last month, but honestly I'd written about so many shady mining practices in the paper by then that it could have come from anyone, not just from this tarot-sending menace . . .

I'd written about so many shady mining practices.

I should have seen it before. After all, I'd been doing it on purpose. I'd *wanted* to stir the pot.

Turned out those little silver cards had been stirring *my* pot all along!

I stood up at once. "I have to go."

"Fine," said Saki, her voice mild. "Take your macaron for the road."

* * *

I ate the cookie in two bites as I charged up the path that led to the mine. I had to hand it to Glacial—the macaron was pretty good.

Silly as it was, that bit of sugar took some of the edge off my anger. Because of that little cookie, I didn't burst into Lark's office shouting and waving tarot cards, at least. I'm not saying that's *exactly* what my intention had been when I left the café . . . but I will say that if I had, Lark's henchmen would probably have thrown me out on the spot.

Instead, I rushed into the office and found Lark, her secretary, and the two large trolls who served as her bodyguards all in deep conversation.

Lark herself was gorgeous, as always. She ruled the room from behind a large desk, which obscured most of her magitech wheelchair. The way her long wavy hair shone aquamarine, and the way her eyes matched it, always tried to distract me with thoughts of the beach, of warmth and relaxing . . .

"Leo," she said briskly, seeing me by the door. "What excellent timing you have."

"What happened?" I snapped back to business. Though I glanced at the secretary and trolls, their grim expressions told me nothing.

"A decision," said Lark. "I am going to—temporarily—move my headquarters."

"Move?" I repeated. It felt silly, but there was no way around it. "To where? Into town?"

That would actually be a *wise* decision, given how she and her business had been threatened over the past year. But I knew Lark too well to hope for it. Lark was brilliant at running her mine. She'd built her empire up from nothing.

And like my granda, she never turned up her nose at a risk if she saw profit on the other side.

"No. Farther away." This time she didn't look at me.

I stomped up to her desk, ignoring the trolls. "Are you—are you *running?*"

"I am not." Her eyes flashed as she met my gaze again. "I am making the right decision for the sake of my company. If you must know, my silver mining operation has suffered several attempts at sabotage. This morning there was a fire in one of the tunnels. No one was hurt, but—it is time to take a different approach. The mine itself is at the base of the mountain—too far from my current operations. So I will make sure I am present where I am needed most.

"All of that is strictly off the record," she added.

For once, I wasn't even thinking of the story. Belville was halfway up the mountain. The mountain was huge. To shift her headquarters to a branch operation at the *base* of the mountain—she'd be at least a day's travel away. In fact, she'd be . . .

"Where?" I asked abruptly.

Lark's lips curved up, ever so slightly. "You've reported on everything my company has done, Leo. Surely you know where the mesmerized silver operation is."

I did. It was the same place my "cease and desist" had come from.

"You're not letting her go to New Dale?" I asked the trolls, the secretary—anyone else, in fact.

"It's not a question of anyone letting me," Lark said firmly. "It is already done. I leave tonight."

"But the cards," I protested, pulling them out of my pocket. "Did you see them—did you see yours? The *fire* on it?"

Lark looked steadily at the card, then up at me again. Her face was resolute. "My choice is made."

I knew it was futile. There was nothing I could say to her— nothing that would change her mind. Not even if it was my brightest idea yet. And as her words hung in the air, I felt the

terrible pang of an incoming ending.
Sometimes, risks and rebirths come too late.

***

Card Reader

A Leonine Investigations Mystery
Elle Hartford

9

Cheating at Cards

A good investigator is always one step ahead of the police.

If my granda knew how the police were banging down my door at the print shop, he'd be turning over in his grave.

Nyx, the black winged cat, went flying over printing presses as the knocking continued. She darted into my office and perched atop a cabinet of back issues of the newspaper, hissing.

"I'm going," I muttered, effectively shooed away from my desk.

But I didn't make it far. As I crossed the shop floor, the door opened. My assistant, Maggie, came up the stairs with Officer Thorn behind her.

Maggie, short and elf-like, wore a knit sweater, a knit cap over her short silver hair, and a strained smile. The kind some people put on when they *know* their news is not going to be received well. Officer Thorn, six feet tall with mossy green skin and long black hair, wore her uniform and a stern expression.

"I told her not to bother knocking," Maggie said, "since it's my time to come in anyway, and I could just bring her up with me, but she wouldn't listen."

"This isn't just a social call," said Officer Thorn.

"Thanks for the warning," I said. I stood between the rows of printing presses, arms folded. "Tell me you got all the charges against me dropped just as forcefully."

"You haven't been charged. Yet." Officer Thorn gave me a pointed look. Her specialty. Aside from being loud and stubborn, that is. But as the sole officer in a small mountain town, I could see how she might need those qualities.

My granda always warned me that the police and the press are like cats and dogs. Same goals—most of the time—but different methods. I didn't dislike Officer Thorn, but we'd had our share of disagreements. And when it came to the strange tarot cards I'd been receiving, and the following threats of legal action if I continued to expose shady mining practices in my paper . . . Let's just say that was the biggest disagreement of all.

Big enough we needed a mediator. Maggie hung her scarf and bag on a hook near the door, and then got down to business. "Leo, Mina just wanted to make sure you knew about some, um, some bad news from New Dale."

I tugged my good hand through my wiry mess of curls. The morning had been cold, and I hadn't bothered with the brass magitech prosthetic for my other hand yet. Instead, I clutched my arm close to my side. "Is Lark involved?"

Lark, local mine owner and another one too stubborn for her own good, had set up temporary headquarters in the fancy town at the base of the mountain barely a month ago.

"No, *you're* involved," Officer Thorn said, moving into the shop until she rested one elbow on a press. "Or that is, you'd better not be. I was talking to my friend down at New Dale station last night, and he mentioned that your *friend* has been especially proactive lately."

I was confused. "Lark?" We weren't friends. She never listened to me. If it weren't for the fact that we'd both been receiving anonymous tarot cards all year, we wouldn't have anything in common at all.

"No, the people who sent you that official warning over the summer," Maggie said.

I glared at Officer Thorn. "I thought you said you couldn't pin down who it was. Even though you *insisted* I leave the investigation to you."

"We can't pin any crime or public record to them, but we know who they are, all right," said Officer Thorn. She tossed her hair over her shoulder. "My friend is the one who dealt with them when they lodged the official complaint against you. But he couldn't say anything about it, officially."

"And now?" I prompted, gritting my teeth.

"Now, I can tell you, with special emphasis," Officer Thorn said slowly, "that the Silver Grail Mining Company just pressed charges against a former secretary in New Dale for stealing documents."

"Harsh charges," Maggie said. "And there's not even conclusive proof that the secretary is guilty. Right?"

"Right," Officer Thorn—Mina, to her girlfriend Maggie—confirmed. "The New Dale police station is doing its best to be neutral, but the Silver Grail folks have been in town a long time, and they're . . . aggressive. That's the word my friend used."

My mind raced. What documents could be so precious? What had the secretary seen, or overheard? What new level of corruption could be uncovered there? I shook my head. "So?"

"So," said Officer Thorn, firmly, "you're staying right here in Belville, got it? And I recommend your next issue of *Belville & Beyond* focus entirely on the upcoming Halloween fair."

"You can't order me around," I said, frowning. "I haven't done anything wrong!"

"I'm not ordering, I'm preventing you from endangering yourself."

"I'll endanger myself all I like!"

"Not on my watch, you won't!"

Officer Thorn and I stared each other down. I knew I was in the right. But she was easily twice my size. And blocking the door.

"Um," said Maggie. "This might not be the best time, but . . . Leo, we noticed these envelopes sticking out of the mailbox as we came up."

* * *

Of course they were tarot cards.

I'd snatched the envelopes from Maggie and stormed into my office, but Officer Thorn hadn't taken the hint. She'd followed me, and Maggie had followed her. Now the three of us stood crowded around my messy desk. Atop edited articles and mining reference material and a string of paper bats I hadn't gotten around to hanging up, the two plain envelopes sat.

And atop them, two new tarot cards.

"This was the one addressed to you?" Officer Thorn spoke as she picked up one of the cards. It was a glossy black thing, just like all the others, embossed in silver. *VIII: Strength*, it read, accompanied by a line drawing of a lion. "I see the resemblance," she added, glancing at me with a wry expression.

I kept my mouth clamped shut.

"That means this was the one meant for Lark," Maggie said, looking at the other card. "I wonder if it was forwarded on from her new office? Or if it went to the old office, and someone there knew to send it on?"

"Do you think it matters?" Officer Thorn softened as she looked down at Maggie's bent head.

"Of course it matters," I burst. "It means the tarot card sender knows where she is."

"I can't imagine that's difficult to find out," Officer Thorn said, the wryness back in her voice. "Anyway, I don't see anything on the envelope that would answer the question. No postmark, just a handwritten note, 'forward to Leo,' as usual. I could go up to the mine this afternoon and check—"

"*I* could," I interrupted. "It's *my* mail!"

"That's as may be, but this is getting too—"

"Don't say it!" I warned.

The three of us stared down at the tarot card.

Dangerous. The unspoken word hung in the air.

The tarot card for Lark glinted darkly in the low office light. *XV* was its number. A set of manacles was its illustration. And its caption: *the Devil.*

"This just proves everything I've been telling you," Officer Thorn said.

If her girlfriend hadn't been standing between us, I might have punched her. Or sicced Nyx on her, at least.

But Nyx was asleep on the cabinets by now, and Maggie was distracted. "It makes me think of something," she said, reaching out. Officer Thorn shifted as if she might swat her hand away from the card, but quick as a cat Maggie gathered both cards up and went to the cork board in the corner.

There, all the cards Lark and I had received had been neatly arranged, by Maggie herself. My cards were pinned in a row above, while Lark's were pinned one by one in the row below. Maggie held this *Devil* card up to Lark's row. "See?" she asked, looking back at us.

Officer Thorn looked at me and I ignored her. But I had to admit I had no idea what Maggie was getting at.

"The Devil," said Maggie, shaking the card. "It's scary, right? Like a lot of Lark's cards have been. She got Death, back in May, and just last month she got Judgment, which also was very dramatic, with its phoenix and the whole idea of something dying in order to make way for something new. Don't you see? Lark has been getting all the scary cards!"

"I got the Hanged Man right at the beginning," I protested.

"But that's really just about inevitability. Saki told us that," Maggie reminded me.

I crossed my arms again. "Not having a choice is scary!"

"You're missing the point," Officer Thorn told me. "Maggie's right. Lark's the one I'd really be worried about, looking at those pictures. Even the Moon one is unsettling."

"Try telling *Lark* that," I said. "I've been trying since the beginning. She won't listen to reason, not even when her precious deals fall through and her ores get stolen!"

"This Devil one reminds me of handcuffs," Officer Thorn said, as though I hadn't spoken. "Somebody getting locked up, maybe. On second thought, it might not be a bad thing . . ."

Maggie shivered. "It would be for the poor secretary in New Dale."

"But this card is for Lark, not them," I said.

Officer Thorn turned to me. "Have you thought that maybe Lark is behind them all?"

I gaped. "Is that your idea of some kind of Halloween prank?"

"It doesn't make a whole lot of sense," Maggie said, more carefully. "Why would she sabotage her own company? Why would she incriminate *herself* by sending herself the Devil card?"

"We don't have any proof she received the card," Officer Thorn pointed out. "All we know for sure is that it's put Leo in a tailspin. Maybe that's what she wanted."

"I am not!" I drew myself up and swiped the envelopes off the table, taking the cards from Maggie. "I am perfectly rational. And I'm going to check with the mine about the card right now. Alone!"

* * *

It was raining fitfully on the mountain. That was fine. It matched my mood.

I pulled my rain slicker close as I went up the rocky path to the mine. So Officer Thorn wanted me to forget all this and just focus on the Halloween fair in town, did she? And no doubt she'd happily see Lark behind bars!

I was just about ready to run down the mountain to New Dale myself. Town holidays be cursed.

And yet . . . What was the company name she had given me? Silver Grail Mining Company. That would need some looking into. A good reporter always prepared before an interview . . .

When I arrived at the mine, I was just shy of prepared. I paused for a moment. My breath puffed, white clouds in the damp air. Lark might have moved herself and her main staff down the mountain, but a barebones crew still operated this mine. I watched them disappearing into mine tunnels, carts of ore rolling out. In the center of it all was the shabby little wooden office building. Lark had always preferred practicality to looks. She liked to be in the thick of things.

And so did I. I trudged across the muddy ground.

When I got to the office, it was a troll who met me in the front room.

"Skar?" I was surprised. Normally the hulking hench-troll, one of a pair, was never far from Lark's side. "What are you doing here?"

"Watching over the mine," the troll said simply, in a voice as deep and gravelly as the mountain itself. "Skaab and I. We are in charge."

"But what about Lark?" I demanded.

"Lark said stay here," Skar told me. "And trust no one else."

"I won't argue that you're trustworthy," I said, setting my hands on my hips. It wouldn't get me far to insult a troll. "But *what about Lark*? Who's looking after her?"

"Secretary," said Skar simply.

I wanted to scream into the void. All this talk of secretaries was too much. But at least it reminded me of my mission. "Skar, did Lark leave you instructions about the mail?"

"The mail?" said Skar, thinking it over before nodding. "Send the mail on."

"To me?"

Skar blinked. "Why you?"

"I didn't mean *all* the mail. Just the—" I tugged the tarot card and envelope from my coat pocket. "Just the ones like this. Did you see a letter like this in the mail this morning?"

Skar looked at the plain white envelope for a long minute. "The handwriting is familiar. Lark's secretary wrote that."

"But you never saw it?" I said, giving the envelope an

impatient wave.

"Just saw it now," said Skar.

"But this morning?"

"No." Skar spoke decisively. "Not this morning."

"And not yesterday?" I had to cover my bases. Who knew if the letter had taken time to re-deliver?

"Not ever before," said Skar.

"Thanks," I said, thrusting the envelope back in my pocket, where it crumpled. "You could've said that at the beginning, but never mind. That's all."

I turned to go, but hesitated. Over my shoulder I said, "If you hear from Lark . . . Don't tell her I talked to you."

Skar watched me go. I was positive that the troll would spill the beans at the first opportunity. Lark would probably know about my visit within the hour.

But what did that matter?

Strength. That was apparently my omen for the month. If that was the case, then so be it. I smiled grimly as I walked out into the fog.

Regardless of anything Officer Thorn said, I was going to continue with this case. I was going to unmask this menace. I was going to New Dale.

Just as soon as the silly town festival of candy and ghosts was over.

* * *

Cheating at Cards

A Leonine Investigations Mystery

Elle Hartford

10

A Run of Cards

I never understood the "damsel in distress" thing until I *was* one.

Tied up at the bottom of a well outside of New Dale, a town where I knew no one and no one was about to come looking for me.

I'd really made a mess of things this time. And the irony was, I had tried to be careful . . .

* * *

It started in Belville. Like all things do. The Halloween fair was over, snow was on the forecast, and my bag was packed. I was all set to hitch a ride to New Dale to confront Lark.

Of course, before I'd even crossed the town square, Nyx flew after me with two envelopes in her claws.

I waved the black cat away. She had plenty of food left out for her at the printing shop. The last thing I needed was for *her* to get involved with vengeful mining companies, too.

Alone and with a pit in my stomach, I opened up the

envelopes, one at a time. The morning sun glinted off the silver etchings. Two black tarot cards. *XIV: Temperance,* with liquid pouring between two cups for me. *XI: Justice,* with an imbalanced scale, intended for Lark.

I broke into a run.

* * *

One long omnibus ride later and I was in a new city. New Dale was at the bottom of the mountain compared to Belville, but the clouds hung heavy over the gray buildings. Most people on the cobblestone streets kept their heads down. A passing coach splashed through a puddle and drenched my bag.

I'd done my share of traveling. Even though I'd never been to New Dale before, I knew how to start my visit. Taking care to make sure I wasn't followed, I found an inn and engaged a room for the next few nights. The innkeeper and his staff were chatty, but as informants, useless. They hadn't heard anything noteworthy coming from the nearby silver mines.

I had to scope out a few different pubs before I found one full of miners. From the sound of it, many had just finished their shifts and come back to town for the night. Perfect. I took a seat at the bar and waited.

It was early yet to start drinking, and I knew I'd need a clear head anyway. I asked for a hot cider and sat nursing my mug until someone shoved up next to me and took an interest.

She was broad-shouldered and gray-skinned, her black hair pulled back in a tight braid. "Not many tourists find this spot," she said by way of hello with an easy grin.

"I'm in geology," I said, just as easily. I'd settled on a good backstory on my way down. Sometimes, a little bit of subterfuge was the only way to get ahead. "Just got a full professorship, believe it or not. But I've always been more comfortable in places like this, that remind me of my student days. Call me MJ."

"Moth," my new friend replied, reaching out to shake hands. "A nickname the team gave me. You teaching here in town?"

"No, I'm just here to scope out field trips—and collect samples," I said, testing the waters. If Moth was involved in shady mining practices, she wouldn't be too happy with anyone sampling and testing the ore she helped retrieve.

"I get it," she said, smiling. "You're looking to get in with Gail."

I hesitated. The bar was loud, and I wasn't entirely sure what she had said. In all my reporting so far, I hadn't run across any person named Gail . . .

But Moth hadn't shut the conversation down yet, so I decided to press on. "Isn't everyone?"

"Sure. Comes with being the top dog," Moth said, chuckling. "But Gail tends to play things close to the chest."

"I heard another big name recently got to town." I watched Moth carefully as I added, "Lark, from Belville Mine?"

Moth shrugged. A raucous customer bumped into her shoulder, pushing her into me for an instant. "New discoveries always bring newcomers sniffing around."

I took a drink to buy time to think. I couldn't quite be sure what she'd said. *Discoveries,* that seemed right; I couldn't imagine what else it would be. She was still smiling. She waved away some friends without looking away from my face.

"You haven't seen her around, then?" I asked. I tried to sound casual, but curse it, I'm a reporter, not an actor. And the room was going cloudy. "I have a—message for her—from a fellow professor."

"I haven't," Moth said. My gut immediately said she was lying. But my head was spinning. "We Gail folks stick together."

I leaned in. What had she said? It didn't make sense. I looked down at my empty cup.

Then it clicked. Moth wasn't saying "Gail," she was saying "Grail."

As in Silver Grail Mining Company.

The "top dog" in local mining . . . Who had, naturally, sent me cease and desist letters over the summer, and had recently made the news for trying to sue a secretary just for *thinking* of spilling company secrets. Close to the chest, indeed.

That's the moment I knew I had pushed my luck a little too far. *She had put something in my drink.*

And when I looked at my companion, my stomach dropped. She could see it in my face. I saw it in hers.

"Why don't I take you to her?" she asked, her friends closing in behind her. "Anything to help out a new friend."

Darkness was closing in. I was outnumbered and outmaneuvered.

This wasn't going to end well.

* * *

I sat on the cold wet rocks in the dark and went over it again and again in my mind. There wasn't much else to do.

I'd gone from reconnaissance to kidnapped in the blink of an eye. What really got my goat was that I could see how it happened. The exact moment I'd gone too far. I'd asked about Lark directly. I'd shown my hand. And what I'd thought was a set of straightforward cues had turned out to be a trap.

And now I'd woken up to find I'd been trussed up and abandoned—escorted down into an old mining shaft and left there, who knows how far underground. In the gloom I could barely tell that the elevator was gone, the control panel smashed.

There was a chance I'd be found if a mining team came here to work in the morning. But what good was that? My quarry would be long gone by that time. There was no way I'd get close to Lark or the Silver Grail now. Any quips about "taking me to" anyone had just been salt in the wound. I'd been utterly transparent.

More than the ropes and the darkness, it was the hopelessness of it that weighed me down.

I kicked a pebble into the shadows. I was all out of options. There was no one left to turn to.

Another pebble went skittering away from my foot. The true helplessness of being "in distress," I decided, was not physical: it was knowing you had no other recourse.

My boot made contact with a larger rock. I kicked it and it made a satisfying *thunk* against the far wall, but the feeling was fleeting.

Then I kicked another, bigger rock. This time there wasn't a thunk. Instead, there was an ominous creak.

"Who's there?" A muffled voice demanded.

Tied hands or no, I scrambled to my feet. "Lark?"

"Don't be a fool," retorted the muffled voice. "I know you aren't Lark."

I could have cried. Instead, my mind was racing through the facts. Moth hadn't been lying—not about everything. They really had decided to hide us in the same place. Maybe it was their idea of a joke.

"Keep talking," I directed. "I'm going to find my way to you."

"You'd think the Silver Grail would arrange more than one mine shaft to dump its enemies into, given the rate at which it accumulates them," said Lark, dryly. I followed her voice, walking in the same direction the rock had gone. In the darkness, I ran nose-first into an earthen wall.

Fortunately she was still talking. I could hear her a little to my right. "Perhaps it's a matter of convenience," she was musing. "This way, there's only one area to keep the police away from. Perhaps it's a matter of neglect and poor planning. I will say I have not been impressed with their organization so far. It took them until this very morning to even confront me. Assuming I'm right about how much time has passed . . ."

Her voice trailed off as I found a door, shouldered it open, and found her sitting in an old office lit faintly by luminescent moss.

"For the record," she said, tossing her hair, "I knew it was you. Otherwise I wouldn't have bothered talking."

"You knew it was me because you told them to put me down here?" I asked cautiously, willing my heart to slow down.

"Yes, and I told them to put *me* down here for good measure, because I like your company so much," Lark said sarcastically. But after a beat, her face softened. "What's a reporter doing down a mine shaft anyway?"

"I was about to resign myself to writing my final story on the walls," I admitted. "But now I know that you're here, I doubt I'll get any peace. We may as well try to escape. You haven't got anything on you as sharp as your commentary, have you?"

Lark was seated in a decrepit wooden chair. I'd assumed her arms were tied, like mine, but she smiled wryly as she waved her hands at me. "They thought I'd be useless without my

101

wheelchair," she explained. "Come here. If my nails can't saw through the knots, you'll have to settle for me untying them."

I did so, amazed that anyone had underestimated Lark like that. As I turned around and she began tugging at the ropes, I said, "In return, I can carry you out."

"As appealing as that offer is, it won't be necessary," Lark assured me. "My ride will be here any minute."

There was a faint rumbling, deep within the mountain. I shook my head. "Of course. You called the trolls."

"A good business owner always communicates with her employees," said Lark, smugly. "And she always has a back up plan. Those thugs didn't even notice my spare communication spell. If *I* was going to abduct someone, I'd make sure my minions knew how to conduct a search."

"The cards," I said, reminded by her talk of communicating. "They came this morning, to Belville. You got Justice."

Lark's answer was chilled. "Not yet. But I will."

The ropes loosened, and I turned around to face her. "I got Temperance."

Even in the gloom, I could see how her eyebrows rose in amusement. "You don't smell like you've been very temperate. Made some friends in a pub, did you?"

"In retrospect, maybe it *was* meant as a card of moderation," I confessed. "But I didn't learn my lesson, and I don't intend to learn it now. I'm coming with you. You can't stop me."

"I could if I wanted to, but I don't," said Lark, as the rumbling grew closer. "In fact, I want you to witness the entire thing . . . so you can set it down for me later."

I reached out for her outstretched hand and shook it, nodding as I said, "In stone."

The far wall began to break.

Whatever had begun with that first tarot card months ago was about to come crumbling down.

* * *

A Run of Cards

A Leonine Investigations Mystery

Elle Hartford

11

Draw!

Snow was falling softly outside my window. It was the worst.

The worst because I'd been in New Dale for a fortnight and had nothing to show for it. Nothing, that is, except a certain hot-tempered mine owner for a roommate.

"We need to try something," said Lark.

I turned away from the window. "What do you suggest that we haven't already tried?"

"Anything!" she said, frustration clear on her perfect face. "As long as we keep moving!"

Easy for her to say, especially in that fancy chair of hers. My feet were killing me. My everything was killing me. I was beat.

Two weeks ago, I'd stormed into town and found Lark on night one. (Okay, there was a slight mishap there—but we're not talking about it.) When Lark and I busted out of the mine shaft where we'd been left to rot, she had been full of big talk about taking the fight straight to the bad guys: Silver Grail Mining Company. But that hadn't gone as planned.

Turned out, the Silver Grail Mining headquarters were

locked down tighter than a drum. Not even Lark's hench-trolls made a dent in their defenses. Then the police showed up and wanted to know what *we* were doing disturbing the peace. It wasn't pretty.

We went round and round for a little while. Us accusing Silver Grail of kidnapping, intimidation, and corrupt business practices, them accusing us of slander and libel and anything under the sun. Pretty quickly we reached a stalemate. No matter who might be paying them bribes, the police wouldn't arrest a reporter without evidence—especially a reporter as annoying as me. And I was plenty annoying, particularly when they confiscated my notebook and magical recording pen. I never got them back, but I put up quite the fight.

And that's not even mentioning Lark.

"I will *not* give up and go home," she said.

This had been her refrain, nonstop. Ever since the police gave us up as bad business, she'd insisted we get more evidence and make our case again. That meant we had to get into the Grail headquarters. Which as I already mentioned were locked up tight.

Not that we hadn't been trying. When the brute force of two trolls hadn't worked, we tried just about anything else we could think of. Dressing up as mine employees. Smuggling ourselves inside delivery boxes. I'd even tried outright applying to be a secretary there, which lasted about two seconds. Not even magic had worked.

I paced the inn room we'd been sharing. Lark could probably have afforded her own place, if you ask me—after all, she did have her temporary headquarters in town still, and none of her things had been stolen—but she hadn't insisted on solitude.

"It's almost Yule," I said. I was tired. And for once, I was actually feeling nostalgic for Belville. Market Square was always a sight in the snow and holiday lights . . .

"Exactly," said Lark. "It's almost Yule. Everyone's distracted with holiday spirit."

"So?"

"So, can't we use that to our advantage?"

I glanced back at Lark, sitting calmly beside our one end table, and caught sight of a half-eaten piece of cake by her elbow. In that moment, inspiration struck.

"You know what?" I said, coming to a halt, "I think we just might."

* * *

In two shakes of a reindeer's tail, Lark and I were at the gates of Silver Grail Mining Co. Her only attempt at disguise was a corsage of poinsettias pinned to her lapel, but luckily she was hidden behind the towering cake box in her lap. I wore an apron, glitter face paint, and a knitted cap complete with reindeer antlers.

"Who goes there?" asked the burly woman inside the booth.

"Cake delivery," I said, as cheerily as I could muster. "From the New Dale Improvement Committee, to every single one of Silver Grail Mining's employees!"

The guard's magitech intercom crackled. "Really? What kind of cake?"

At first my mind was blank. I hadn't really expected some glitter and a hat to get around their facial recognition spells. But then, the guard wasn't even looking at me.

Holiday spirit, indeed.

"Six varieties," said Lark next to me. "Chocolate truffle on the bottom, then cranberry cream, spiced vanilla, drunken rum cake, peppermint dream, and a premium aged fruitcake on top."

"Fruitcake, you say?" The buzzer crackled again. "The employee cafeteria's on the third floor to your left."

Just like that, the gate swung open.

"Wait a minute," the guard called, before we could walk in.

I turned on my heel. "Yes?"

"Your visitor badges," she said. Two lanyards appeared beneath the booth window. I grabbed them as quick as I could and walked on.

We were in.

* * *

We were in, but we didn't make it far. In fact we didn't make it past the lobby.

Employees were coming out of everywhere. I swear I saw one walk through a wall.

"Cake? Did someone say cake?"

"I need a dairy-free slice!"

"I want a piece of spice cake!"

"I told my office I'd get them all a piece!"

I had to bodily push one away from Lark. I almost kicked another.

That's when Lark's flair for being in charge kicked in.

"Everyone, remain calm," she said. It didn't sound like she was yelling, but her voice was so loud everyone else fell silent. "Due to safety restrictions, cake will be served only from the cafeteria on the third floor. As this is a special holiday presentation, we require extra time for set up. We appreciate your patience. Once the cake is ready, everyone will get a piece. Happy Yule!"

"Happy Yule," the employees chorused halfheartedly. But it worked. They began to drift away.

Not wanting to press our luck, I hurried Lark into the nearest elevator. As the magical door slid closed, leaving us alone, I said, "Do you mean to tell me that while I was out getting a disguise, you actually bought all that cake?"

"Of course. Cake should never be a lie," Lark said calmly. "Third floor, please."

"No way am I getting bogged down in serving that much cake. We have a detour to make first," I said, pushing the button for the top floor. No evil business owner could resist putting their office on the top floor.

"Fine."

After a minute, as our platform whizzed upwards, I said, "That was pretty impressive."

"Thank you." Lark smiled to herself. "I've probably never told you, but I once had my own headquarters raided."

"What?" That was news. How had I not heard it?

"Back in the old days. Officer Thorn, and her friend the alchemist, though they failed to take away anything too damaging to the mine." Lark's smile became a smirk. "I learned a thing or two."

We didn't have time to get into what she learned. At that moment the elevator stopped, and the door slid open.

"Right on time," someone said. "I was just about to put on a kettle of tea."

Lark stopped dead. "Gerry?"

* * *

Who in Beyond was Gerry?

When Lark and her cake box finally got out of the way, the pieces fell into place. We emerged from the elevator into an office that took up the entire top floor. It was more of a suite— as I looked around, it became clear that someone might live there. Potted plants, sofas, white tile. Not a holiday decoration in sight.

There were, however, three people visible in front of us. Two stood beside a massive wooden desk. The third, a slight man with light hair, was sitting behind it. As he smiled at us, I realized why Lark knew his name. He was her secretary! Or— had that been only a pose?

"I sent you back to Belville to watch after the mine," Lark said, wheeling forward.

"More like, to be watched by your trolls," said Gerry, dryly. "When did you begin to suspect me?"

"I'm always suspicious. It comes with the business," Lark replied. She set her cakes aside and glared at him, cold as ice. "But I didn't expect you to be so high up."

She had a point there. Was Gerry the elusive head of Silver Grail? Running one business while pretending to assist in running another seemed like too much.

Just then, the man to one side coughed. "Gerald is *my* secretary," he said ponderously. He had gray hair and small eyes, and though his suit was tailored impeccably, it didn't hide his weight.

Lark glared at him without compunction. "And you are?"

"Avaricious Silver," said he. "You are sitting in my domain. Welcome."

As long as we were doing introductions, my gaze drifted to the third person—a mousy young woman practically hiding in Avaricious's shadow. "Who might you be?"

110

For a moment, she perked up. "I'm—"

"My daughter is merely observing the proceedings," Avaricious interrupted. "To learn the business, you see."

"The business of putting employees at risk with dangerous mining practices and passing off fake ore as mesmerized silver?" said Lark, her voice hard.

You could have pushed me over with a feather. She didn't even need me there.

"Only a supreme businesswoman like yourself would see it," said Avaricious, ingratiatingly.

"A business owner like myself will do the right thing and turn you in," said Lark.

I sidled closer to her. She was really turning up the heat now. For all our attempts to break into the building, we'd never talked about what we'd do once we got there. I liked a confrontation as much as anyone, but we were outnumbered here. I hardly expected her to throw down the gauntlet so fast!

Gerry was watching me. He must have had the same idea. "Let's take a step back for a moment," he suggested. "I get the feeling you two didn't examine your invitations."

"Invitation—?" Following his gaze, I looked down at my visitor pass.

"I had them waiting for you specially," he said.

My stomach sank. As I flipped the card reading "visitor" over, the room spun. There on the back of the pass was another blasted tarot card.

And mine depicted two people in a close embrace. *The Lovers.*

I couldn't breathe, but I snuck a glance at Lark's. Curious to the last. Hers showed a building struck by lightning. *The Tower.*

Not good. Any way you looked at it, these people were one

111

step ahead of us, thought they knew too much, and weren't averse to violence. Both Lark and I were in for it. This wasn't good at all.

"Of course you were the one arranging the cards," Lark said softly. "That explains why there was never any postmark. You were right there the whole time."

Gerry smirked. "Just carrying out orders."

"What?" Avaricious frowned as he leaned his bulk against the desk. "I never told you to waste time with silly calling cards. Where did you get those? Who did you pay to print them?"

I was as confused as anybody, but it felt good to watch Gerry's smile falter. "But—the instructions were very clear. In my monthly task folder—written down, left here on my desk—"

"Oh, pshaw," said Avaricious. He sounded more angry than careless. "It's no matter now. You'll explain yourself later. We have guests."

"I don't think much of your fraudulent entertainment," said Lark, a hard edge in her voice.

I leaned down over her shoulder. "Listen, I know it's not your style, but if gave them a little more room to talk before throwing out accusations—"

"Listen to your friend!" growled Avaricious.

"A reporter would know," Gerry was smirking again.

"Will you two criminals shut up so we can confer?" I demanded.

The room went quiet.

Lark took the stage, ignoring me. "My, what ringing denials. At least you're honest, Silver. So tell me: what's your next move?"

The man's face was so red he might as well have been steaming. "You want to know? I'll tell you. I'm going to get rid

112

of interferers like you!"

"How?" Lark challenged him, before I could warn her against asking for a demonstration.

"By digging an even deeper hole, and this time throwing you all in from the top!"

The words hung in the air.

"All?" Gerry ventured.

"All you cursed meddlers!"

"But I was only acting on orders—you promised me—"

"I'm done with all of you!"

Avaricious made straight for me, like he was going to the elevator. To call for help, no doubt. After all, he wasn't the kind of person to dig a hole himself! I dug my heels in, ready to fight him.

But before he got to me—

"Thank you both very much for your cooperation," Lark said, using her business voice again. "Ladies, you might want to hold your breath."

Quick as a cat she drew something from her pocket and tossed it on the floor. A heavy smoke billowed up, catching Avaricious mid stride. He only had time for one cough and curse before he crumpled. Gerry fell even faster. Realizing what Lark must have done, I bolted for the window behind the desk and opened it. The mine owner's daughter was at my side, gulping in the clean air. Her hand brushed mine. At the back of my mind, something clicked.

"Vaporized eel poison," Lark said, behind us. There was no mistaking the smugness in her voice. No doubt a coastal elf, a well-connected one at that, had her sources for such things. "You can come back now, it dissipates quickly."

"But Gerry and—Father?" the young woman asked as she

113

turned.

"Inhaling a few breaths of it is enough to paralyze the average person for a few hours, no more," said Lark. "They should be fine by the time we get them to the police station."

"You know, you could tell a person you plan to pull a stunt like that," I said in protest.

"You caught on quickly enough." Lark's expression softened, just for a moment. "But you never seemed to realize that I *needed* to provoke him."

I groaned. No wonder she'd moved the cake box out of her lap. It made for better sound transfer. How had I not thought of it? "A recorder. In your flowers?"

"Of course. I told you I'd learned a lesson last time, didn't I? Always have a spare witness."

"There's one thing you didn't learn," I replied, clinging to my one bit of pride. I turned to the woman beside me. "It was *you* sending the tarot cards."

"Laurea," she said, breaking down at once. She clung to my shirtsleeve with one hand, the other wiping at her face. "My name is Laurea. For victory. I was supposed to take over the company. I've known all along about his plans, but I could never get out. He wouldn't let me leave here! He always just said I had to learn more. But I knew enough! I knew someone had to stop him. I'd read in the papers about you, and Belville Mine, and I just knew—I knew if anyone could do something— you *had* to—I'm so glad—I'm so glad it's over! I'll tell the police everything, the *right* police. I'll stop the bribes. I've got all the evidence you need—just get him out!"

"We'll get you both out," I said, touched by her determination. Turning to Lark, I added, "Looks like we didn't need your recorder anyway."

"Some reporter." Lark grinned. "Hope you're better at cutting and serving cake."

* * *

Draw!

A Leonine Investigations Mystery
Elle Hartford

12

A Full Deck (Epilogue)

J ust days later, Lark and I shared a table at the Pomegranate Café. She'd just finished overseeing the move of her temporary headquarters out of New Dale, and I'd just written up my exposé.

"Of course," I said, "it's more for the people. It's nothing the police don't know already, thanks to Laurea."

"It seems quite flattering to Laurea," Lark remarked, setting down the proof copy I'd brought along for her to read.

I sipped my coffee, grinning. "Why shouldn't it be?"

Lark gave me an unreadable look. "You never did tell me how you were so sure it was her. Process of elimination, I suppose?"

"No. Better." I leaned over the table. "To be fair, it was Maggie who pointed it out first. The really combative cards were always addressed to you—a competitor. Whereas some of *my* cards were downright nice. As if the sender liked me better."

"How sweet," said Lark, very dryly. "Where shall I send the congratulatory wedding flowers?"

I pulled back. "I wouldn't go *that* far." Myself, I'd assumed that final card—*Lovers*—well—I'd immediately thought of Lark. What did that say about me? I didn't want to go too far down that road.

Lark smirked at me, like she could read my thoughts. "Even so, you might be interested in the final letter I got today."

She pulled a plain white envelope from her coat pocket and opened it, passing me a single tarot card.

"Look at you!" Sakura, who was passing by with her arms full of empty mugs, leaned over my shoulder. "That should be the complete set, isn't it?"

"I think it is," I agreed slowly. I tilted the card back and forth, watching the light dance off the silver etchings. *The World*, it read. *XXI*.

The last card. It felt like the most monumental, too. Fittingly enough, the illustration showed a little globe featuring oceans and mountains. I could imagine a tiny mine hidden among them.

"You keep it," said Lark. "I believe it to be a good omen for our businesses moving forward, and that's enough for me."

I looked up. "What if it isn't enough for me, though?"

Lark's smile deepened. "In that case, Leo, maybe you should come over for dinner this Yule."

Bonus Story: Spines of Omission

The following short story is from the perspective of Red—nosy alchemist extraordinaire! It takes place a year or so before the events in The Silver Deck. Enjoy this shifted perspective on Leo, and if you like Red's style, check out The Alchemical Tales books.

* * *

My name is Red, and I'm an alchemist. And while that may sound pretty far out there or even crazy, the truth is, being an alchemist is just like being any kind of investigator: 25% fun tools and science, 25% researching until your head hurts, and 50% wondering how much to trust the things you read and the things you hear.

I never expected that making potions and tinkering with plants and minerals would lead to investigating actual *murders*, though. But as I learned last May, sometimes the things you least suspect have a way of silently creeping up behind you . . .

* * *

"I'm *bored*," declared William, drawing out the words as only an eighty-pound dog-shaped magical creature can.

"I thought you never got tired of spying on our neighbors," I teased him lightly. I didn't bother looking up. I stood at my kitchen island, covered up to the elbows in flour, squinting at an old recipe for periwinkle teacakes. William, meanwhile, occupied his habitual throne—that is, his chosen "spot": the window seat which overlooked our tiny town's Market Square.

"There's no one out," he grumped. "Not even that busybody reporter. It's quiet as a cemetery out there."

"Isn't it bad luck to say things like that?" I reprimanded, ignoring the irony of William calling someone *else* nosy. This time I did look up as I mixed my dry ingredients, blowing strands of long black hair out of my face.

William, however, was not contrite. "At least bad luck is *interesting*," he mumbled.

"Debatable," I pointed out, resisting the urge to point my whisk at him. I'd only have to clean up the resulting mess. Even though we lived in a tiny studio apartment above my potions shop, which theoretically should be easy to look after, I spent enough time cleaning as it was.

"It *is* bad luck," a new, rather breathless voice declared. "Want to go see the traveling aquarium, Red?"

As one, William and I turned to this odd intruder.

Of course, I thought, smiling. *Who else?*

Luca, local bookstore clerk and expert on town history, beamed at us from the landing just beyond the kitchen. Theoretically, he was a scholar-in-training—"scholar" being the term used across Beyond for local historians, who usually owned a bookshop as part of their expertise. But in practice, Luca was more kid-on-a-sugar-high than staid adult. Dressed in long black scholarly robes, his bright green eyes sparkling over dark brown cheeks, he didn't look at all like a terrifying intruder. *Oh—and no wonder,* I reminded myself, *I did leave the back door downstairs open for him, after all. Wow, is it already past noon? I thought he was coming later . . .*

As I realized with horror how my morning had slipped away while I wrestled with this new recipe, Luca seemed to feel the silence. "I—I heard you talking as I came up the stairs," he explained, shuffling in place, his hands tucked behind him as though he hoped to appear small. Given that he was only a few inches shy of six feet, this didn't work too well for him. "Did you know, the common phrase is actually 'quiet as the grave'? And many cultures do believe that to bring up graves and, by extension, cemeteries is to tempt ill fate. In fact, it used to be that even here, in Belville, there was a public ban on—"

William sneezed, interrupting what was promising to be an impressive ramble. "Are you here to literally bore me to death, or are you here to ask Red out?"

"*William,*" I cried, dropping my mixing bowl.

"Oh—no," stammered Luca, his eyes wide as saucers. Flour and powdered petals enveloped my little kitchen in a *poof* as my bowl and whisk clattered against the tile floor. "Um, here, let me help you—"

"It's fine," I protested, despite the fact that I was now covered, from bare copper-colored toes all the way up to pink apron and alchemist's goggles currently serving as a headband, in my latest attempt at a new cake recipe.

That was definitely why I felt like melting into a puddle on the floor. *Not* William's ridiculous assumptions.

"—really sorry," Luca was saying, even though none of this was remotely his fault. He crouched at my feet, gathering the bowl and whisk and really, just managing to get himself as covered in flour as I was. The white dust on his robes made him look like a ghost in a two-bit play. "I didn't mean to ask you out, of course, I mean, I just thought you might want to see it, I mean they just got to town and they aren't even open yet, I think they were worried about press coverage or something? But I know the lady in charge, she's really nice, and she said I could come, and I thought you might want to so that's why I was going to come over and ask you, but then I didn't know you were baking, and I'm really sorry—"

"Enough!" William barked at him. "What happened to you being too shy to talk?"

"*William*," I repeated, exasperated. I was starting to feel like a parrot. For some reason, that thought shook me out of my mortification and made me want to laugh. "I think you're the one who needs to take a break from talking right now. Please."

Luca glanced up at me, and his crooked grin suggested that he agreed with my assessment.

I took a deep breath and smiled back. And then caught myself chuckling. "Okay," I said, running my hand through my hair (having forgotten all about the flour—oops), "let's have a do-over. Why did you ask to stop by, again? What's this about an aquarium? And don't worry about the floor. I'll get it."

Luca stepped back as I grabbed my broom—the one perk of having a tiny kitchen was that most things were within arm's reach—and set to work. "It's my friend, Parker," he told me, as though this made perfect sense as a starting place. In his mind it probably was: most people in the world were friends, to Luca. "She used to be a scholar, like Owl, but now she runs a traveling aquarium. They just got into town last night and they were going to wait until tomorrow to open officially, but she said I could have the first tour today if Owl would give me the afternoon off. And I just thought, you being an alchemist, you might like to see it? Plus she's traveling, like you used to do, and . . ."

William sneezed again, but we both ignored him.

I considered Luca as his voice trailed off. Only a few months previous, I had given up my life as a traveling alchemist and settled in Belville to sell potions, reference books, and scientific doodads. Luca had been one of my first friends in town. I smiled at him. "Sure. I closed the shop today anyway," I added unnecessarily. "We're taking a bit of a break after that weirdness with the carousel horse, and before the summer rush hits. So why not?"

Luca grinned back. He'd helped me with the mysterious carousel horse that had shown up on my doorstep a few days before, so I knew he'd understand why I wanted some down time. And I could definitely understand why he might want time away from his boss at the bookstore. As a scholar, Owl seemed to have more respect for books than for most living creatures.

"We could go now," he said, "if you want to?"

"Just let me change and get some of this flour out of my hair. William—"

"Oh, no you don't," William rumbled. "I'm not staying here by myself. I'm coming with you."

I paused, looking at him askance. "Are you really that interested in fish? They don't talk, you know."

"Of course I know. I'm interested," he said haughtily, "in the two of you having a chaperone."

* * *

123

The three of us descended from my apartment a short while later, once I'd cleaned the kitchen and thrown on a light yellow tunic and leggings instead of half a batch of unbaked teacakes. I kept my goggles on my head because, well, I always do. I'm not afraid of being thought of as a nerd—when you spend most of your time in an alchemical lab or out on the hillsides gathering wild ingredients, "nerdy" just comes with the territory. Alchemy is all about transforming mundane things into better versions of themselves, and I like to think that can be done *anywhere*, so I like to be prepared.

Besides, I was with Luca, who wasn't above a bit of nerdiness himself. It wasn't like I'd have to focus solely on judgy people, like William.

My shop, Red's Alchemy and Potions, sat proudly on the corner of Market Square—the heart and soul of Belville. We crossed the cobblestone street to the green expanse of the Square, walking under leafy trees and past bright May flowers. Businesses of all kinds ringed the Square, including the town's historic tavern, a florist, an antiques shop, and of course, a bakery. Normally the Square was a popular place to meet friends and hang out, but William made a beeline for the one new object on the scene: a large and rather battered-looking caravan.

And while William rushed ahead, Luca and I got jumped.

She appeared from out of nowhere, as though she'd been hiding behind a nearby tree or cloaked in an invisibility spell only seconds before. But I knew Leo was human through and through. Mary Jane Leonine, technically, but everyone in town just called her Leo—it seemed to fit her wild auburn hair, tan skin, and general air of *I'm about to get exactly what I want*. Leo was the owner, printer, and reporter for Belville's only newspaper.

"Nice day, isn't it?" she called to us, her voice fast and arresting. We stopped beneath a maple tree and, as usual, Leo got right to the point. "Headed to the aquarium?"

I looked at Luca.

Luca clammed up.

"Hi, Leo," I said with a sigh. "Yes, we are. Luca knows the owner, apparently. But—"

"Great," she interrupted. "I'll just tag along with you, shall I?"

"You will?" I glanced at Luca, unsure if this was allowed.

Luca cleared his throat. "Um, hi, Leo. Err, yeah—you could come too, I guess. If you want to. William's coming too."

"Oh, I definitely want to," said Leo, sorting through the pockets of her light canvas jacket to come up with a pad and quill. As she moved, sunshine flashed off her right wrist, which was a burnished gold. From the elbow down, her right arm had been replaced by a high-quality prosthetic. But it never stopped Leo; case in point, she seemed already to be framing her new story in her mind. "There's something off about the people at that aquarium," she remarked as she fell into step with us.

"No, there isn't," said Luca, affronted on behalf of his friend.

"Yes, there is," Leo returned. "I'd think so even if I *hadn't* received an anonymous tip this morning."

"An anonymous tip saying what?" I asked, curious.

"Saying," said Leo, with predatory satisfaction, "that someone involved with the aquarium is a criminal."

Luca's mouth opened and closed, like he wanted to protest this. But there wasn't any time, because we'd already caught up with William, who was waiting a short distance from the caravan in question.

It seemed too small to house an aquarium, but there was no doubt that it was our destination: vivid (if peeling in places) paintings of fish adorned its side, and even the wheels glittered with blue lacquer. As a professional, I was curious about those wheels, but I didn't want to fixate on them lest Luca think I was more interested in paint than in his friend's fish. (I might have been.) The caravan was parked under a massive oak, its canvas roof decorated with blue and green ribbons. I had a feeling that if I put on my goggles, I'd see traces of magic all over this traveling aquarium. Normally magic is more William's area of expertise than mine, but I knew firsthand how difficult it could be to keep a traveling business safe and secure. Luca had been right: criminal allegations or no, I already admired his friend's pluck.

The four of us had paused at the back of the caravan, where a series of rainbow steps led to an arched doorway. From behind the nearby tree, two blue heads had appeared.

I forgot all about Leo at once, my mind racing. *Horses. Kelpies?* I glanced at Luca in wonder as the creatures snorted and grazed, completely ignoring us. They looked like draft horses, but their coats gleamed aquamarine.

"At least there's no question they go with the wagon," I murmured to Luca.

He chuckled. "Parker told me all about them in a letter. I think their names are—"

"Sea! Star!" A gruff voice called out, followed by an even gruffer-looking person. He saw us standing by the horses and added, "What're you looking at? Aquarium's closed."

"Oh—I'm here to see Parker," Luca called back, poking his head around Leo's shoulder. But he didn't call loud enough, and the stranger squinted, straining to hear.

Where Leo, Luca, and I all looked reasonably human, this new person was probably part snake. His wrinkled skin was a dark color, almost green in the shadow of the oak, and yellow scales criss-crossed his bald head. He looked like he could have been someone's grandfather, if he wasn't so antisocial. From the way he put his hands on the horses' necks, it was clear that he was the hostler for the aquarium, and he wasn't happy to see us.

He also appeared to be missing one eye. Suddenly, Luca's cheerful afternoon tour of the aquarium felt a little ominous.

"We're here because Luca knows Parker," I repeated more loudly, trying to remind myself not to judge this person. Maybe he lost his eye in a totally peaceful mistake, after all. An innocent aquarium-related accident?

"Huh. Why didn't you say so?" The man didn't move—just continued glaring at us.

Leo tilted her head, her mane of hair ruffling in the breeze. "Does a little aquarium like this really need a bodyguard?"

"'M here for the horses," the man retorted. "Never can be too careful."

This ambiguous answer left us pondering, and in the silence, the caravan door opened. A human woman, perhaps in her late forties and with dyed blue hair, a deep tan, and a broad smile, came out and immediately beamed at Luca.

"You came!" she declared. "And I see you've met Cobra. Cobra, I hope you've been nice to my friends, here? Oh, well. Come in, come in!"

Despite this greeting, Cobra the hostler kept an unfriendly eye on us as we shuffled past him. I kept my lips firmly zipped shut, worried that all my questions—*why can you never be too careful? Are you worried about the aquarium? Are your horses part kelpie? How did you make the wagon wheels so blue? Of all the nicknames in the world, why pick 'Cobra'?*-might fall out of my mouth if my focus slipped.

Before I knew it, though, the caravan door clicked shut behind me, and I was in a different world.

*　*　*

Okay, it wasn't *actually* a different world. But magic was definitely involved in the traveling aquarium, because the inside of the caravan was much bigger than the outside.

Dim, watery blue lighting moved over us from the ceiling, which was murky and indistinct. The floor underneath us was tiled in all sorts of colors and designs—designs, I realized after a moment, reminiscent of ocean corals. The effect made it feel as though we were walking through a reef. Especially because walls of endless glass aquariums rose around us, forming a hallway that turned and disappeared into the depths of the wagon.

And there was no doubt in my mind that Parker, Luca's penpal, had indeed once been a scholar. As the five of us shuffled wonderingly along the path lined with fish, she kept up a constant narration:

"Notice the archway at the beginning? I built it myself. Those are fluorescent jellyfish swimming inside it—aren't they just spectacular? And right after them, of course, we have the pillars of rainbow blennies. I wrote to you about them, Luca; remember I wanted you to research the electric blue variety? Well, I found them! In each of those tanks you'll see a different color. Then to your right we have several kinds of angelfish, always a crowd favorite, though between you and me, they're frightfully hard to keep alive. Always catching colds when we move into a new region.

"To your left there's some more interesting specimens. For example, the alpha fighting fish. You've heard of betas? Well, this little guy can put those to shame! Not only is he aggressive, those spines you see along his back are rumored to be very poisonous. Just one of them could take out a fully grown elephant, they say. And he is very particular. In fact, I'm the only one who can get near this little guy."

Leo drifted ahead as though already bored (despite the fact that she was taking constant notes), and William was still staring, transfixed, at the jellyfish. I joined Luca in peering at the alpha fighting fish, which didn't seem to enjoy the attention. I could have sworn the thing was making faces at me. I took a step back for just a moment, so that I could pull my goggles down over my eyes for a closer look.

"Oh no! Look out!" a scared voice squeaked behind me.

I turned, startled, thinking that somehow the fish had started talking. Instead a pale gnome with brown hair and strikingly blue eyes stared up at me from his full three-foot height. Beside him, on a little gurney, a glass bowl contained a distinctly seasick-looking yellow fish.

Seasick because I ran into them and made the water slosh around, I thought guiltily. *But seriously, where did they come from?*

Aloud, I said, "I'm so sorry—I didn't hear you coming along the corridor."

"It's okay. But we have to be careful because of the *fish*," said the gnome, as though the fish surrounding us were actually minor deities. "This is their home, after all."

He pushed on down the corridor, crooning to his charge. In his wake, Parker said, "That's Niko, my assistant. Most competent nurse a fish could ask for. Caring for sick fish is a stressful job, even for the best in the business."

"If he's the best," mused Leo, pen poised, "why'd that fish look like it was about to croak?"

William made a muffled sound that might have been a laugh, but the rest of us chose to ignore her comment. Parker paused, glancing at us, then seemed to understand: *we didn't ask her to come, she's just stirring up trouble,* I was thinking, and I'm sure that thought was plastered all over my face. Fortunately, Parker seemed as adept at reading people as she was at caring for fish. *A remarkable trait among scholars,* I thought to myself. *Maybe that's why she took to the road!*

"It's hard to fix something when we don't know exactly what's wrong, and the fish can't tell us," Parker continued easily. "That poor chicken fish has given us quite a scare lately. But speaking of fish named after other creatures, take a look at the cardinal fish over here. Her pointed scales just grew in, giving her that 'feathered' look . . ."

Luca shrugged at me, but at least he was grinning. We turned and followed Parker down the hallway.

And down another hallway . . . and another . . . the place was a veritable maze. I tend to get itchy in enclosed spaces if I don't know all the ways out, so I was doing my best to keep track of our location—or at least which direction we were facing— but it wasn't easy. And it didn't help that around every corner there was a trained octopus or a fairy coral or a singing eel. The deeper into the caravan we went, the wilder the creatures became.

"I can see why you wanted to come here," I said to Luca as we stood in front of a crab as big as a wagon wheel. "This place is amazing. And terrifying."

"I'm sure it's perfectly safe, Red," Luca laughed. "And anyway, most of the fish are probably way worse dead than alive. Don't you think? I thought alchemists get a lot of toxins from fish."

"Some, sure," I admitted, "but it's nice to see them alive instead of powdered in a jar. I guess I—I owe you thanks for bringing me along. And everyone else."

Leo was nearby, still taking notes while trying to appear fascinated by a fish with fangs which screamed *venomous,* and William was several paces behind us sitting in front of a neon wrasse tank. His fluffy black head moved back and forth as he watched the fish swim from side to side and back again.

Luca followed my gaze to look at them both, and then grinned again. "It's no problem. I knew Parker wouldn't mind having a bigger audience. She's really passionate about it."

"Who wouldn't be?" I murmured, as the lady in question came over to us, beaming.

"Seen your fill? The exit's right over here. Can you believe we've been through the whole thing?"

"No," I answered honestly, blinking in surprise. Parker reached behind me and opened a panel in what had seemed like a blank, dark wall.

"Feel free to come back any time you like while we're here," she continued, still in her slightly-too-loud tour-guide voice. "The plan is to stay at least a week, now that the summer weather is here, provided we don't run into—" she broke off, swearing, and glared out the door.

How odd. I turned to see what she was seeing.

"Speak of the devil," Parker added, not quite under her breath.

The door opened out the side of the caravan facing the rest of the Square. For a minute, I was baffled more by this than anything else; I'd felt sure we were facing the other direction.

But then I realized what must have made Parker so angry. Right across from the wagon, a small woman had taken over a wooden bench with nearly a dozen hand-made signs. Slogans like *Bad Science Takes Lives* and *No Fish Believes Everything It Ears* (accompanied by a cartoon-like drawing of an angelfish with a large, fin-shaped ear) fairly screamed across the park.

I spilled out of the caravan to get a better look before turning back to Luca and Parker. "Who is that?"

"No idea," Parker ground out in a voice which clearly indicated that she did, in fact, have some clue. Luca looked baffled. Under his innocently worried gaze, Parker sighed and added, "She likes to go by Ann Basilisk, which is a *clear* pseudonym if you ask me. Everywhere we go lately, there she is."

Luca looked at a homemade banner waving in the wind, and then back at his friend. "But *why*—?"

"Beats me," she answered, her voice going terse again. "Come on. You want a drink? I want a drink. Let's end this tour at the tavern."

"Um, it's only two in the afternoon," Luca protested, but mildly. Parker was already striding across the grass.

He caught my eye, and I shrugged. "We may as well, right? I could use a late lunch."

"Where are we going?" William shouldered his way past Gloria out the caravan door. "You're going to see Lavender? I'm coming too."

"Why don't we all go," Luca said, looking around and finally up at Leo.

William and I agreed at once, but Leo, I noticed, was silent. Her eyes were fixed on the protest signs. Instead of joining us, she stashed her pen and pad.

"Leo?" I asked. I'd never seen her let go of a story opportunity

132

before.

"I know her," Leo said quietly as William and Luca strode off without us. "We were at school together."

"So do you want to go say hi?" I asked, still puzzled.

"No," said Leo, very quietly. Then, squaring her shoulders, she said, "I bet it was her who sent me that note. I *thought* the handwriting seemed familiar. I better go check it out. Don't bother waiting for me. Just be glad you got to see the aquarium," she added, tossing the words over her shoulder as she set off across the grass, "before we shut it down."

* * *

Lavender's Tavern is nothing if not welcoming, no matter how many sea-monster fish or agitating signs you've just seen. One of the largest single buildings in Belville, the tavern sprawled along one corner of the Square, with flowers spilling out of window boxes and vines climbing up the pillars supporting its wraparound porch. The upstairs level hosted guest rooms, while the downstairs was a fine restaurant and bar. Now that the weather was warm, the tables out in front of the tavern were almost always full of people talking, eating, and laughing.

Together, Parker, Luca, William, and I actually managed to have a decent lunch. We took a seat inside, where there was sure to be shade from the afternoon sun. Lulled by the clinking of glasses as Lavender cleaned up from the lunch rush, and the warm scents of herbs from the kitchen, I soon forgot about the strange shock of Ann's protest and Leo's warning. And by the time we'd finished our burgers and sweet potato fries, and Parker had had a flagon—or three, everyone else seemed to be feeling genial, too. In fact, as we got up to leave, Parker was downright affectionate over Luca and me. I decided not to mention Leo's strangeness; it would only spoil the fun.

That brightness lasted as we all parted ways and William and I returned to my apartment. I had just enough ingredients left, I decided, to try my teacake recipe again.

Just as the light outside my windows was beginning to wane, and the teacakes were cooling and William was napping peacefully, my mind fell back to Leo and Ann Basilisk and the aquarium. If anyone was going to expose a criminal, it would be Leo. Why she'd never left Belville to take down a massive city crime ring or expose a massive dragon fraud or something of the kind, I'd never figured out. What was it about Belville that kept the interest of a reporter like that? And furthermore, what interest could she really find in a traveling aquarium? Unless Sea and Star were secretly sea nymphs in disguise or the whole operation was a cover for drug smuggling, I really didn't see what could be so illegal about it.

But that was about to change.

A sharp knock sounded at the door below. Through the wood and up the staircase, I could hear the official voice ring out:

"Red! Look sharp! I need your expert opinion on a matter of poison. There's been a murder!"

* * *

Small towns all across the world of Beyond rely on the support of specially-trained members of the Police Guild, which dispatches recruits only after they've been fully trained in all sorts of things ranging from settling petty disputes to capturing the attention of crowds to detaining known criminals. And Officer Thorn had been *born* for her role.

Belville's resident officer (the town merited only one officer, who lived above the squat little station on the edge of the forest), Thorn excelled at all the things her Guild asked of her. Since she was at least half-orc and therefore green-skinned, very broad, muscly, and a head taller than the average human, most disputes tended to die out quickly once she arrived on the scene. With perfect bearing and a booming voice, she not only captured attention but demanded it. And nothing seemed to bring her more satisfaction than ordering people around—whether those orders were of the detainment variety or not.

She collected William and I with practiced ease, and shepherded us out to the Square—to the caravan, in fact. And in a second, she had us all following direction as if we'd practiced this for days.

"This" being a murder. I shuddered.

"The victim is still in place," said Officer Thorn. I followed her gesture toward the old oak tree and saw Luca, and for a moment my heart stopped. But, no: he was standing, and perfectly fine, if a bit worried-looking. Looking more closely, I saw that there was a lump at his feet. No doubt Thorn had caught him walking round the Square and told him to guard the murder scene while she fetched me.

"Name, Ann Basilisk. Cause of death, poison. It's pretty clear where the poison came from," the Officer was saying, "but I want you to be the one to collect the spines, since you're the expert. But that'll keep for just a minute. First, take a look at this one, here."

"This one" at first seemed to be another crumpled form laying on the grass just shy of the caravan steps. I recognized Parker immediately, and the rise and fall of her chest assured me she was alive. As Officer Thorn hovered, I went and crouched at Parker's side.

I'm not any kind of doctor—I prefer inanimate subjects—but I knew enough roadside first aid to help Parker rather than hinder her, and fortunately I had a water bottle in my bag. I offered her some as soon as she came to.

"It's not—it isn't—it's nothing to do with the aquarium," Parker insisted woozily as she tried to sit up.

Ooookay, sure, totally normal first words for someone regaining consciousness, I thought, but I didn't voice my skepticism aloud. "We don't know that yet," I said, trying to be reasonable but also sound reassuring. It didn't work too well. "Here, can you drink a little water? Try to take deep breaths."

Parker took the water bottle, but her breathing remained irregular as she looked around at the circus which now surrounded her caravan. "Is she *really* dead?"

"It sounds like it. Officer Thorn just did a cursory examination," I said, thinking, *now* there's *a more reasonable concern.* "Just focus on regaining your strength for now."

"Maybe she did it to herself," Parker muttered.

This seemed uncharitable in the extreme, and I was going to rebuke her when I noticed the look on her face. Up close, even in the twilight, dark under-eye circles and sagging lines around the mouth made it clear that Parker wasn't just struggling with the news—she'd been struggling, maybe exhausted, for days on end. I wondered if it wasn't shock but fatigue that had brought on the faint in the first place.

From the other side of the caravan, I was pretty sure I could hear William and Cobra the hostler yelling at each other. Officer Thorn cocked her head and listened.

"I'm glad you brought him along," she said to me, no doubt

referring to William. "I *knew* I hadn't found all the aquarium people yet. Come on. You collect those spines, I'll collect the witnesses and the body. Then we're all going down to the station."

The body, I thought, biting my lip. *What a tragedy. And on top of that . . . it looks like this is going to be a long night.*

* * *

"It's going to be a long night," Officer Thorn declared, "so make yourselves comfortable. Red! You're up first. In my office, if you please."

I sighed. The station's front room, usually bare except for scattered chairs and maps lining the wooden walls, now overflowed with the aquarium staff and my friends. Or, as Thorn probably thought us, *suspects.* I glanced meaningfully at William, hoping to convey a message to *sit here nicely and don't provoke anyone,* as I followed Officer Thorn and shut her office door behind her.

Like her uniform, Officer Thorn's office was immaculate. She sat behind the heavy oak desk and tugged at one pointy ear, tossing long black hair over her shoulder. Finally, she said,

"I *told* the Mayor we shouldn't give them a permit to set up in the Square without doing an investigation first."

"The aquarium people?" I clarified, dropping into one of two chairs opposite Thorn. "Luca knows them. Well, he knows Parker, the owner. He seemed to think they were totally fine. Unfortunately, it was the sign lady—Ann—who seemed to be stirring up trouble."

The Officer grunted. "Luca thinks everyone's 'fine.' What do *you* think?"

I glanced at her—then at the door behind me, and the waiting room beyond—and then back at her. "Is this part of your interrogation?"

"Don't be ridiculous, Red. You aren't a suspect. You're helping the police by providing valuable insight," she informed me with a toothy grin.

I pressed my own lips very tightly together to resist the urge to chuckle along with her. This wasn't the first time Officer Thorn had insisted I act as her "unofficial assistant," and seeing as she was so short on help, I understood her thought process— I really did. But that didn't mean I *enjoyed* being dragged into these situations.

But Officer Thorn, despite her impulsive nature, can be incredibly patient. And stubborn.

Finally I admitted, a bit reluctantly, "Well, I think you were right about those spines being the source of the poison, first of all. I have them here." I held up a glass sample bottle with four cherry red spines inside. "And I have to admit, if I wanted to murder somebody, there were plenty of ways to do it in that aquarium. The alpha fish, for example, was known to be poisonous."

"Is that where those came from?" Thorn asked, nodding at the bottle as I set it on her desk.

"I'm not a fish expert, so I can't say for sure. But it's possible," I said.

"And there was one of these 'alpha fish' in the aquarium?" When I nodded, she continued, "It shouldn't come as any shock to you, Red, that I'm thinking this was an inside job. Inside the caravan, that is."

"It did seem like tensions were running high in there. I get the feeling they'd been traveling hard—maybe even 'on the run,' so to speak, from Ann," I admitted. "Have you talked to Leo?"

"The reporter? No. Why do you ask?"

"She was there earlier—she toured the aquarium with Luca, William, and me. She said she'd got a note about a criminal working out of the aquarium. And," I recalled, eyes widening, "she said she'd gone to school with Ann."

"Then we better find her," Officer Thorn decided. "But I need to get statements from everyone here first. Tell me more about the tour you took. Luca was there, you say?"

"And William and Leo," I added hastily, omitting the fact that Luca had really only asked *me* if I wanted to go. Aside from that small white lie, I filled Thorn in on everything I could remember.

"Right," she nodded, "so that means you were heading home around three, three thirty. And I discovered Ann's body myself this evening on my rounds, just before seven."

"And Luca?" I heard myself asking. "Why was he on the scene?"

Officer Thorn shrugged. "Said something about wanting to deliver a thank-you note to Parker. Makes a lot more sense now that I have a coherent story from you. Of course, when he and she came down the caravan steps and saw me and Ann, that's when the faint occurred."

I nodded glumly; so far, everything held together.

"So," Thorn continued, sitting back, "we have you, Luca, William, and Leo-currently MIA. Then there's Parker, Cobra, and Niko. And Ann, of course. Checked into Lavender's Tavern last night under the name Ann Basilisk, so that checks out. Not much in the way of belongings, though, but she had some fancy jewelry—much nicer than her clothes. Speaks of new money, if you ask me. She had a whole host of anti-aquarium brochures in her pocket, but nothing else."

"No evidence of criminal activity?" I asked.

"None. But she might have hidden it, or given it to Leo," said Officer Thorn. "We definitely need to find that reporter. And you said the spines came from an alpha fighting fish?"

"I said I'm not sure. But Parker did tell us that fish was very poisonous."

Well, she'd said it was *rumored* to be poisonous, and Ann had accused the aquarium of bad science. *Is this what she meant?* I quickly added, "But there were tons of toxic fish in there, so really, Parker ought to know better than me. The alpha fish just happened to be one of the first ones we saw, right by the front door."

Officer Thorn grunted. "So it was accessible. That opens up the suspect pool. Ha, pool, get it? But really, any one of them could have reached in and grabbed a few of these."

"They'd have to be very quick," I said, doubtfully. The aquarium tanks had opened in the front, so theoretically what Thorn said was true, but I couldn't imagine catching a live fish. "Why don't you try looking at the fish in the aquarium to see who's missing spines?"

"And how would I know which ones are missing spines when I've never seen any of them before?" Thorn asked, one eyebrow arched. "I'll be asking Parker, don't you worry. She and I took a quick sweep through the aquarium while you were gathering spines and your dog was convincing Cobra to come along.

"And besides," she continued, "the murderer had to be quick anyway to catch Ann unawares like that. She used to be a marine biologist, did you know that?"

"No," I said, frowning. "How did *you* know that? Come to think of it, why do you already know so much about Ann?"

"Because," said Officer Thorn, leaning conspiratorially over her desk, "I ran into her last night at Lavender's, and she invited me up to her room herself. Wanted to ask me all about Belville, and how things work here—especially the newspaper. Turns out, she wanted to know all about Leo."

* * *

"So," William whispered, as we huddled together guarding the waiting room while Officer Thorn interviewed Luca. "Whoever is the criminal in the aquarium had strong reasons to kill Ann."

I shifted uncomfortably. I'd filled him in on Officer Thorn's revelations as quietly as I could, but it still felt weird to talk about everyone while we were in the same room. Fortunately, Parker seemed oblivious, and her employees were about as far from us as they could get.

"We just have to figure out which of them is most on guard," William continued.

"True," I whispered back, "but don't they *all* seem strangely on guard? Except Luca, of course."

"Yeah. Maybe Ann just strayed too close to that guy Cobra's horses," William said, his tail thumping against the floor as he thought.

"Maybe we should try a different angle," I said after a moment. "Officer Thorn thinks we *all* had access to the alpha fighting fish, but I'm not so sure. Cobra and Niko both had their own duties to tend to, and Parker herself made it a point to say only she could touch it."

"Or someone quick and desperate could," William suggested, sounding awfully like Thorn. "Leo was pretty interested in the dangerous fish."

"Why would Leo kill someone who was giving her tips?" I asked, my eyebrow raised.

"Maybe they had some sort of blood feud going on," William whispered, "and the aquarium thing was only a cover. Or maybe Ann was blackmailing Leo!"

"Now you're just being maudlin—"

Behind us, Officer Thorn's door opened and Luca stepped out. He looked around the room, finally smiling weakly at us. "Parker," he said, uncertainly. "You're next."

"Parker," repeated Cobra, much more loudly, as he elbowed his boss. "Get in there."

William and I exchanged a look. Maybe there was more than just one feud and one secret behind this aquarium after all.

* * *

Officer Thorn's interview with Parker went on for a long time. She called Cobra in next, and at the same time sent me out for some pizza from the Square. On my way back, I ducked into my shop to grab a reference book on fish.

And as I emerged from my back door, hands full of pizza and an old encyclopedia, a shadow wavered on the patio.

"It's just me," said Leo, quickly.

"Gods and goddesses," I swore, trying not to drop anything. "For goodness' sake, why are you here? You should be at the station, you know."

"I *don't* know," she said, and she sounded rather bewildered at having to admit such a thing. "What's going on? I came over here to ask *you*."

I set aside the question of why she felt more comfortable

coming to me than going to the police station, and I set down the pizza boxes on the edge of a potted plant so I could lock my door. "Leo," I said, not looking at her, "there was a murder. Ann Basilisk. Officer Thorn found her just a few hours ago."

This time, it was Leo's turn to curse.

I turned around and really looked at her. The evening starlight illuminated her face well enough, and the emotion in her voice seemed genuine.

"You said you knew her?" I asked, more gently. "I'm sorry to be the bearer of bad news."

"In college. It seems like ages ago now," said Leo, though I doubted she was more than thirty-five. "I was supposed to meet her. Tonight, I mean. She had something to tell me—but she only wanted to talk about it in secret, in her room at the tavern."

"So you don't know what this could be about?"

"Obviously it's something to do with the aquarium," Leo replied at once, "but I don't know who, if that's what you mean. She wouldn't say. Just that someone there had a history of running scams and even selling fish on the black market, and she had the receipts to prove it."

So much for Officer Thorn's hope that Leo could crack the case wide open, I thought. But something else occurred to me, too. "If she had all the proof, why was she hanging on to it? I mean, why expose them now, in Belville? Why hadn't she stopped them before?"

Leo paced my small patio, her green eyes distant. "She came from some kind of ancient noble family—the kind who were always trying to stay out of the paper. Honestly, I was surprised she wanted to talk to me at all. But maybe *that's* why. She knew she could trust me."

143

"Well, either way," I said, not wanting to pass judgment on Leo's trustworthiness, "we'd better get you to the station to talk to Thorn. And I better get everyone their pizza before it gets cold."

* * *

As Leo and I entered the station, Cobra came out of Thorn's office. "Sure," he muttered, seeing me, "she lets *you* go out. What are the rest of us waiting here for?"

"For safety," said Niko, in a thin, soft voice.

"Just in case," Luca agreed, coming to help me set down the pizza boxes. "It's not so bad. She just wants to make sure that whoever it is doesn't run—"

Cobra turned his back on us. "Like *I'd* run. It's all the rest of you who are running *here*."

This didn't make too much sense, but he seemed unwilling to elaborate. The rest of us shrugged, and turned to our dinner as Thorn called in Leo next.

"What book did you get, Red?" Luca asked, sliding into a chair next to mine with pizza in his hand.

"I should have known you'd be interested. Keep your cheese away from it," I laughed, removing my book to safety on my other side. "It's a reference guide for tropical fish. I've had it ever since we did a trek along the coast."

I thought it might help confirm or deny some of these fish facts— and therefore, alibis, I thought, but did not say in a room full of suspects.

But Luca was excited anyway. With his non-pizza-y hand, he began paging through the book eagerly.

"Hey, Parker," he said, stopping at a page-long section about sharks, "did you know—oh." He paused, and Parker hadn't turned from her chair by the door. "I should have remembered," Luca murmured to me, "she wrote me once about how she doesn't hear so well from one ear. Water damage, I think she said. Parker!" he tried again, louder, and this time managed to get his friend interested in his find.

Hum. Water damage, I thought, sitting back. That certainly explained some of Parker's behavior, which had seemed surly before. And did it explain why Cobra was so protective, too?

My head throbbed as I tried to puzzle it out. *The only thing I know for sure,* I decided, *is that fish tanks are a lot more dangerous than I thought.*

In my beleaguered state, the thought tickled me because it wasn't exactly true. It wasn't as if, had all the fish been in jars instead of tanks, anyone in the aquarium would be any safer. In fact, they'd be much worse off, because whenever the caravan moved there'd be water all over the floor.

Sloshing water. The image made me pause. Why? Was it because I thought it possible that maybe Ann *had* reached into a fish tank of her own accord, grabbed the deadly spines, and then stumbled out of the caravan before dying? No—that didn't seem right. It was something else I had seen . . .

"Alright, listen up," Officer Thorn declared, coming out of her office with Leo in tow. "It's time we review the case together.

"First of all, it looks like Ann *did* die of poison—from a red fish's spine, to be exact. And some of the only things she left behind were essays and pamphlets directed against what she called the 'dishonesty' in the aquarium. This *specific* aquarium. But since no one has anything to say about that," Thorn continued, with a pointed look at Parker, "I'm left to suspect whoever had best access to one 'alpha fighting fish.'

And that is *you*."

"No," shouted Cobra, standing, as though he would fight Thorn before she cuffed his boss.

"But it's true," said Parker, in a sort of whisper-shout. "He *was* missing spines."

"This is going too fast," protested Luca.

"Just let her do her *job*," said Leo.

"Why would a biologist be mad at a scholar?" barked William.

Officer Thorn looked momentarily shaken. "Could you all just settle down?"

I glanced down at my book, which Luca had discarded. Crumbs had fallen between some of the pages, and absently I shook them out. Accidentally, I turned to an image of a bright yellow fish.

And I thought of Parker's story, and her words just now. *It's true.*

"No," I said aloud, standing to capture everyone's attention. "It *wasn't* true!"

"What now?" asked Thorn, tugging hard on her ear.

I lifted the book to show her—to show everyone.

A bright yellow fish with red spines.

Spines rather like a rooster's comb.

"The spines didn't come from the fighting fish," I told her. "I was mistaken. They came off the chicken fish—which, according to the book, is the deadliest fish of its size."

Across the room, Leo frowned. "You mean that little fish we saw in the bowl in the hallway? It didn't have any spines."

"Yeah," I agreed, thinking of that water sloshing, "and it didn't look very good, either, right? I imagine it'd be pretty tough for a fish to have its spines clipped off!"

"But what about the elephants?" asked Luca, eyes wide.

"A story to throw us off track, maybe?" I looked at Parker.

And, to be honest, I felt a moment of doubt. If Parker had wanted to misdirect us about the fish, why would she have misdirected us to one that she admitted she knew best? And why clip the spines off *two* fish to cover her tracks, when she so clearly cared for them all?

Meanwhile, Parker seemed enveloped in a quandary of her own. She murmured to herself, just loud enough to be heard by everyone, "But Niko said it was having trouble growing them in the first place . . ."

As one, we turned to the corner to see what Niko would say. But Niko wasn't there.

In the stunned silence, the front door banged open. We all leapt to our feet. My blood was pumping, anticipating a chase. Any minute, I knew, Thorn would start yelling. But the very next sound was—

A very loud *OW*, which reverberated through the station as the would-be escapee ricocheted back from the doorway. Niko flew backward, colliding with William, who fell into the table, sending pizza flying all over the room. Just in time, I snatched the book back to my chest. Luca, however, was a little too slow. He got a slice of cheese and tomato right to the face.

In the greasy, confused aftermath, Officer Thorn grinned widely.

"And that is why it pays to have spells that stop people from bolting out of doors without permission," she declared.

* * *

One week later, Luca and I helped Parker pack up after a successful stay in Belville.

"Just check to make sure the tanks are latched," she said, marching up and down the dim hallways. "And the hermit crabs need a cover, otherwise they get scared. Same for the tetras. The zombie piranhas need some extra food—*where* did I put it?"

She stopped, her head tilted to one side as she tried to remember. I caught Luca's eye and tried not to laugh.

"We'll help, but we can only help with things we know," he told Parker, winking at me.

"I know, I know," she sighed before smiling back at us. "This whole 'not having an assistant' thing is harder than I remember."

"I heard Niko confessed and that he's going to trial," I murmured. "I'm sorry."

"*I'm* sorry about the whole mess in the first place. Especially for the poor alpha fish. And the chicken fish, come to think of it. I never realized what was going on," Parker said. "I hired him because of his experience with breeding tropical guppies. I was so grateful for the assistance, I didn't look into him the way I should have."

"You couldn't have known," Luca said reassuringly.

But Parker shook her head. "I should have put two and two together. I was just always focused on the fish. Ann only showed up *after* Niko got here. I assumed she was after *me* about the cages, the traveling, you know—things being bad for the animals. But it turns out, she was after Niko, due to some shady dealings he'd done in the past. She lost all her family's money and her reputation on some fish investment scam— that's what the reporter told me. And then she just wanted to make him face the truth, I suppose. But he . . ."

"He couldn't stand the exposure," I finished for her, sympathetically. *But it got him anyway.* Leo had done some excellent work in the past week, uncovering Ann's hidden evidence and drawing connections between Niko and a larger ring of black marketers on the coast. Word around town was she was even going to spend her summer tracking the rest of them down, in honor of her friend.

"Well, it all makes sense, at least," said Luca. "Even if it *is* pretty terrible. But you and Cobra will be okay."

"That we will." Parker's eyes gleamed fondly, and she hesitated before turning back to work. "I never would have guessed it, though. Niko was always so . . . unassuming."

"If William were here, he'd say it's the quiet ones you have to look out for," I said, in an attempt at a joke.

"Oh, I don't know. Some of them are pretty cute," said Parker. My heart skipped a beat before I realized she was gesturing at her fish tanks. *Oh, right. Fish. Fish are quiet. And . . . cute?*

Across the hallway, Luca winked.

Bonus Quiz: How Noir Are You?

Our number one reporter, Mary Jane Leonine, is a noir character in a cozy world. She takes herself seriously and stares shadows in the face. Sometimes that's a good thing, leading to cases closed and treachery unveiled—and sometimes it just perpetuates the drama!

But how about you? Read on for a tongue-in-cheek, light-hearted take on what it means to be *noir*. From classic mysteries to modern-day intrigues of politics and futility, "noir" is a brand of tense storytelling that does have its allure. Find out how much you align with this stark way of thinking by answering the questions below:

1) The best kind of weather is . . .

   A. a beautiful sunny day to share with friends

   B. not too hot, not too cold

   C. the rainier the better

   D. I never notice the weather, but somehow it is always pouring.

2) I work best when . . .

   A. I can collaborate with others and get positive feedback

   B. I get a chance to organize my tasks

   C. I'm left completely alone

   D. I'm on my own, don't know who to trust, and there's a

monster—or possibly the government?—breathing down my neck.

3) After a hard day's work, I treat myself by . . .

    A. going out for a fun evening with friends!

    B. having a quiet, relaxing night in

    C. moving straight on to the next task

    D. downing a drink that tastes awful and staring out into the blackness.

4) In my opinion, the glass is . . .

    A. Half full!

    B. Too big.

    C. Half empty.

    D. probably about to get crushed by the wayward, destructive hands of fate.

5) My favorite tarot card is probably . . .

    A. The Lovers

    B. Temperance

    C. Death

    D. The Fool, because we're all fools on a long, hard journey and at least in the beginning we have naivete to keep us going . . .

How did you do?

Tally up your answers: 1 point for each "A," 2 points for a "B," 3 points for a "C," and 4 points for a "D." Once you have your number, find the range it fits into here:

5-9 Points

You're not noir. But on the plus side, you're probably a) not sick from trudging around in the rain all the time, b) often in good company, and c) a lot more fun at parties!

10-14 Points

You could be just a little bit noir, but more likely, you know the value of some quality alone time. Keep up the self-care work to balance out all that practicality, and you'll be fine.

15-19 Points

It's hard to tell if you're noir or just overworked. Give yourself a break once in a while, and you'll find things looking a little more cheerful.

20-25 Points

You're pretty noir. Congratulations?

About the Author

Elle adores cozy mysteries, fairy tales, and above all, learning new things. As a historian and educator, she believes in the value of stories as a mirror for complicated realities. She currently lives in New Jersey with a grumpy tortoise and a three-legged cat.

Find stories and more at ellehartford.com. And while you're there, sign up for Elle's newsletter to get bonus material, behind-the-scenes sneak peeks, and goofy jokes!

Also by Elle Hartford

The Alchemical Tales series (cozy mystery meets fairy tales)
   The Carousel Capers (free prequel)
   Beauty and the Alchemist
   Cold as Snow
   Mermaid for Danger
   Cry Big Bad Wolf
   Cinders to Dust
   Death Pulls the Strings
   A Thousand and One Alibis
   Tangled Up in Murder

Pomegranate Cafe Romance (sweet romance novellas)
   Worthy in Love
   Strong in Love
   Steady in Love
   Sweet in Love

Marine Magic (cozy fantasy goes to the beach!)
   How to Care for Cursed Fish